Manoj Kumar Panda writes stories and translates between English and Odia. He has three short-story collections to his credit—*Hada Bagicha* (Bone Garden), *Varna Bagicha* (Alphabet Garden) and *Maya Bagicha* (Garden of Illusions). He received the prestigious Sarala Award in 2015 for *Maya Bagicha*.

Snehaprava Das retired as principal of the B.A Government College, Berhampur. Her work includes translations of *Padmamali* and *Bibasini, A Historical Romance*, the first two Odia novels, *The World Within*, the first psychological novel in Odia; and *Prison Poems*, a collection by Utkalmani Gopabandhu Das, famed social activist, freedom fighter and educationist of pre-Independence India.

ONE THOUSAND DAYS IN A REFRIGERATOR

+ STORIES +

Manoj Kumar Panda
Translated by Snehaprava Das

SPEAKING
TIGER

SPEAKING TIGER PUBLISHING PVT. LTD
4381/4 Ansari Road, Daryaganj,
New Delhi–110002, India

Copyright © Manoj Kumar Panda 2016
Translation copyright © Snehaprava Das 2016
First published in India in paperback by Speaking Tiger 2016

ISBN: 978-93-85755-73-6
eISBN: 978-93-85755-71-2

10 9 8 7 6 5 4 3 2 1

Typeset in Minion Pro by SÜRYA, New Delhi
Printed and bound in India by Thomson Press India Ltd.

Author
For Manju, of course

~

Translator
*For my beloved parents, the only two people
who have loved me unconditionally and unselfishly*

Ultimately, literature is nothing but carpentry…
With both you are working with reality, a material
just as hard as wood.

—Gabriel Garcia Marquez

Contents

When the Gods Left

RAJULA DIP SPENT thirty years of his life disposing of dead bodies. He would carry away carcasses of dogs, cats, pigs, cows and bulls; he sometimes had to pick up unclaimed corpses, too. He would be summoned whenever dead bodies were found lying on roadsides, on railway platforms, or in the beggars' colony. Rajula would transport the corpses to the cremation ground. He was particularly efficient when the police, the municipality, or somebody with an inclination for philanthropy extended financial help. Whenever he would drag a body to the cremation ground, he hoped to receive an extra five or ten rupees for his efforts. His prayers would sometimes be answered. But on most occasions, the man in charge would scribble on a chit of paper and hand it over to him. On presenting this, he would get a bottle of liquor. His hard work was worth that much, at least.

There was once a time when Rajula would come directly home after collecting his bottle, and he and his wife would share it. After the liquor worked its magic, Rajula would hold the bottle over his head and sing and dance. If Rajani, his wife, protested, Rajula would silence her with his shouting. When Rajani got drunk, she would start throwing kitchen utensils at her husband and attack him with sticks, bamboo staffs, glowing logs from the hearth, metal ladles, kitchen spoons—whatever she could lay her hands on. It would usually be midnight by the time the fight ended. Later, when both of them were aroused, they would pull at each other's hair, tear each other's clothes off and roll around on the bare floor.

The following morning, on opening the door, Rajula would find a sober, shy morning waiting for him—an innocent morning, one as guileless as his own smile.

It had been years since Rajani Rani had left this world. When she died, Rajula Dip had addressed her fondly: 'My old wife, you know we are untouchables. Our mortal remains will not find their way to the Ganga or the Godavari. They will go into the gutter. Go, my dear, may your soul cross all gutters on its way to the other world. I will follow you soon and we will resume our jobs. You will sweep away dirt, clear garbage, and I will get rid of carcasses.'

Rajula Dip had lived a lonely life for many years.

~

The night was still young when someone knocked on Rajula's door and told him to reach the Padhihari house in Nuapada by five in the morning; the family cow had died. Having done his job, the man left as suddenly as he had come.

This was exciting news. Old Rajula dragged his ramshackle trolley-cart to a lamp-post nearby and set about mending it under its feeble light. The base of the trolley had three large holes, the body was rusted all over, and the wheels, too, had come off. Still, Rajula began with enthusiasm. He had not been able to find a dead cow for ninety days. As a boy, Rajula used to help his father on such assignments. In those days, if everything went smoothly, they would get five or six rupees from a cow. The hide fetched two rupees; the bones went for half-a-paisa per seer and the flesh for four paisa a seer. Prices had now gone up. The skin brought one hundred and fifty rupees. A kilogramme of cow-flesh cost ten rupees and a kilogramme of bone cost one rupee. When everything went well, Rajula would make nearly two hundred rupees out of each dead cow. But it was one week of hard work.

Rajula Dip was over sixty. His freckled, gnarled skin, cracked feet, balding head, the stringy veins which snaked up from his feet all the way to his neck, his rib-cage—a bamboo mat clearly defined underneath thin skin—the dark navel bored deep into his belly, his drooping ears—everything bore the mark of age. Several burns, scars of healed blisters and old wounds gave Rajula's skin the look of a tyre-tube with hundreds of punctures sealed up with patchwork. Everything about Rajula was old except his eyes—they held a child-like innocence and a bright smile. It was incredible that someone's eyes could carry so much humility and so many dreams at once. Even a teenager's eyes could not measure up to them. His eyes never reflected the disappointment of not being able to find a single dead cow in ninety days.

People envied his laughter—frank, open, expressive and imperious to such a degree that it created an impression of omnipotence. As if he was all in all, supreme, absolute! He was shapeless, formless, all-pervasive—it was as if he was God himself!

There was something very natural about the way he laughed, free of any artifice whatsoever. His laughter flowed like an undercurrent in the depths of his being. He laughed as though he had stolen the laughter from everyone else's lips and hoarded them in his own.

Rajula had two passions: sleeping and dreaming. He would sleep most of the time, and dream. In his dreams, he would pick up dead animals and carry them off on his trolley. He would see a throng of customers in front of his house—people who had come to buy cow-hide, cow bones and meat. He would weigh the flesh and bones and sell them. Sometimes he would make a profit of ten rupees, sometimes twenty.

When he is paid ten rupees in place of twenty, he only smiles. He smiles, dreams and sleeps—this is all he likes to do. He sleeps and he dreams. He dreams that he is sleeping, and in that sleep he dreams again. In this dream he sleeps again and dreams once more. Like Chinese boxes—a small box; within it, a smaller one; a still smaller one inside the smaller box and yet another inside it.

Rajula Dip was now mending the wheels of his rundown trolley-cart, wheels which had not rolled for ninety days. The rusted hooks and nails had come off the axle. Rajula Dip fixed them with the help of ropes. It was quite late by the time he finished. Silence reigned; the street was lonely and the neighbourhood dark. Old Rajula, his trolley, his sleep and his dreams seemed to be the only entities populating that noiseless world. Rajula went off to sleep near his trolley in the middle of the street.

Early the following morning, a group of people passed by. They looked at the sleeping Rajula. The old man has died in his sleep, they thought. But their footsteps and their whispers woke Rajula. He rose to his feet and began pushing the trolley-cart. He was aware that he had to cover a distance of four kilometres. There was a municipality tap on the roadside; he thought he would rinse his mouth and wash his face, but dismissed the idea when he saw a few women standing nearby. He noticed that runoff from the drains had collected and formed a small pool on the roadside. Rajula washed his face and eyes. The touch of the cold water was refreshing; a soft, cool wave rippled over his body. His wet moustache and thick eyebrows looked rough and bristly. Suddenly, he smiled at some thought that crossed his mind. The glow of that smile hung on his lips when he resumed his long walk to Nuapada. Rajula closed his eyes as he trudged along and memories came flooding in.

He had left home after a fight with his parents. He had been very young then. After trying his luck here and there for a year or so, and after having gone hungry most of the time, Rajula finally found work as a guard at the main gate of the king's palace. He worked there for four long years. That was a crucial phase in his life—a turning point. It was then that he fell into the habit of sleeping and dreaming. He also met Rajani Rani when he was working at the palace as palace guard and fell in love with her.

Once he was appointed, Rajula was given a gun and a khaki uniform. He was also given a large sheet of cloth, which he still had, though time had punched several holes in it. Layers of dust had accumulated on the sheet and bugs had made their home in it; it was now thick and heavy, like a blanket. Rajula sometimes said to the bugs, 'Where are you running away? Are you playing hide-and-seek with me? Just you wait, I will teach you a lesson.' Rajula Dip would pick out the bugs and squeeze them to death. He would then wipe his bloody fingers on his blanket and say triumphantly, 'See, I got you, didn't I?' He would talk to the new bug which had put in an appearance: 'You want to suck my blood, eh, you rascal? Are you trying to threaten me? You're finished, I tell you. Run, run for your life! See if you can save yourself.' Sometimes the bug would escape Rajula's pursuing fingers and he would say, 'You are lucky; you got away today but tomorrow is another day.' He would then draw the blanket over himself and fall asleep.

Working as a guard did not entail too many hardships. He was to note the names of people who came to meet the king and turn them back on some pretext or the other. 'The king is resting, he cannot see you now,' he would say. There were men who would not accept such excuses. Rajula would point his gun at them. But the funny way in which he held the gun would amuse the visitor rather than frighten him. The man would end up teaching Rajula the correct way of pointing a gun at someone. Yet no one would approach Rajula—people found the idea of touching him repulsive. Rajula realized that the fear people had of brushing against him was more of a deterrent than the gun. If he reached out and tried to touch someone, the man would immediately rebuke Rajula and leave, forgetting his audience with the king.

Even after serving four years as a security guard, Rajula never set his eyes on a bullet. He could not tell butt from bayonet. Sometimes, he would hold the gun upside down, the pointed end piercing the ground, and sleep with his cheek resting on its butt. But no one, not even a kitten, would venture to walk past the sleeping Rajula. People feared his touch more than they feared his gun.

The king gave Rajula a salary at the end of every month. He would drop three one-rupee coins into Rajula's outstretched palms. On occasion the king would just throw the coins on the ground and Rajula would pick them up. After picking up the coins, Rajula would wait for the king to order him to leave and would not budge until the order was issued.

Rajula was given a small, rickety bench to sit on while he kept watch over the main entrance. At night, Rajula slept on the bench. The nails that joined the wooden planks would come loose every now and then and the planks would start to buckle. The legs, too, would threaten to come off. Rajula would fix them, using a large stone to drive the nails home. Sometimes he would use a long rope to hold the planks together; at other times, he would wedge the branch of a tree under the bench. To keep the bench leaning against the wall was another alternative. Still, whenever Rajula sat or slept on the bench, he would do so with the utmost caution. Even then, Rajula had managed to fall off the bench no less than eighteen times in four years; his clothes had been ripped by the loosened nails at least eight times. The bench had soaked in rainwater and warped. Rajula developed a chronic backache from sleeping on the uneven surface. The nails would prick him all over his body and make him miserable. Still, Rajula was very fond of the bench and took good care of it. He even talked to it at times. 'What will your plight be when I am not around?' he would ask it good-humouredly. Rajula did not speak only to the bench. He would also address his gun in a voice suffused with emotion.

It was during those days that he met Rajani Rani. Rajani Rani used to walk along the southern boundary

of the palace at a fixed time every morning, carrying a
bucket on her head. Rajula and Rajani observed each
other for a long time and smiled at each other from a
distance. After a few more days, they saw each other up
close and smiled again. It took very little time for them
to bridge the distance. They met at the palace gates
and smiled at each other. Then, they smiled at each
other in Rajula's lonely room. Their growing intimacy
manoeuvred the smile to their eyes, to their lips, to their
skin and the flesh under it. Like a virus, the smile entered
their livers, their lungs, their sweat and their blood and
travelled through the private zones of their bodies to
reach Rajani's womb. They smiled at each other's dreams,
at each other's speech and silences. They laughed at the
smoke-stained walls and the black cobwebs, they laughed
at their own shabby appearance and the thinning hair on
their heads; they even laughed at all those things which
pitilessly exposed Rajula's poverty—the tattered mattress,
the old blanket on which bugs played hide-and-seek, the
broken bench, the gun, the threadbare mats, the soiled
socks hanging from a nail in the wall, the old shoes with
their ripped-apart soles. They laughed at the onion peels
and the blighted rice-grains scattered here and there on
the dirty floor.

It took the king two months to learn about Rajula
Dip's relationship with Rajani Rani. He sent for Rajula,
flung four one-rupee coins at him and ordered him to
leave the palace. The king sent a man to collect the gun

from Rajula's house. Rajula and Rajani were forced to leave town.

All of these incidents took place nearly forty years ago. The memories seemed almost unreal.

~

It was not yet morning, the old man walked along the road, pushing his trolley-cart, his eyes closed in sleep, his mind wandering in the forbidden terrain of the remote past. All at once the wheels came off with a thwack and Rajula was jerked awake.

'What happened, my child?' he asked. 'Another breakdown? How many times will I have to mend you? How long can I take care of you?' Rajula sat down to fix the wheels.

'Please bear with me this one single day,' he implored the trolley. 'There will be no problems from tomorrow and you can sleep as long as you like. But don't fail me today. Remember how many times I have helped you—it's your turn now. I haven't found a dead cow in ninety days. You know I have been going without food for so long. Can I look after you or feed you in this condition? You know that my old woman has left me alone in this world. I have grown quite old myself, and so have you. It will soon be time for us to make our exit. Help me just this once. Help me carry the cow home, just this one time. Never again shall I trouble you.'

Finally, the wheels fixed, the trolley began to roll

again. Rajula pushed it along and finally reached the Padhihari house. The sun was rising. Everywhere he looked was bright and clear. The soft, golden light of the nascent sun flickered on the rustling leaves of the tree. Old Padhihari motioned Rajula to move along to the back of the house. Rajula did as he was ordered. The big cow lay on its back, one of its hind legs raised vertically towards the sky. The cow was black. A broad white line like the trunk of an elephant ran down the entire length of its belly. On its forehead was a patch which looked like an octopus.

Rajula Dip rarely spoke to human beings. But he readily spoke to carcasses, to plants and trees, and to inanimate objects like his blanket; he talked to the bugs in the blanket, his shoes, his clothes, his trolley-cart, the door and the walls of his house; he spoke to cow-dung, the soil, the green meadows and the sky. He liked to talk to his own hands, his own blood, his wounds and even to the temperature of his body when he had fever.

'How long do you intend to keep me in bed? How can I feed you unless I get well and go out to work? Mind you, if you do not leave my body by tomorrow morning, I will go out to work and leave you here.' Astonishingly, the temperature would come down the following morning. When old Rajula would get ready to go about his work, pulling the trolley-cart along, Rajani Rani would stop him, 'There is no need to go anywhere today. You have been down with fever these last three days. You must be feeling weak.' She would catch hold of the handle of the trolley-cart and push it into a corner. Old Rajula would flop down on the verandah without objection. These were all memories from the distant past. It was almost a decade since the old woman had died.

Rajula walked around the dead cow once and wondered where to start. A couple of farm hands who ploughed Padhihari's land sat close by. Rajula asked them for a beedi. They threw him one. Rajula sat smoking for a while. He then flung the remnant of the beedi as far away as he could and started roping up the carcass. First tying the four legs together, he pulled the trolley close to the cow. He wedged a thick branch under the wheels of the trolley and tilted it so the rear edge touched the ground. With the help of a pair of strong bamboo staves, he levered the cow up on to the trolley-cart. This took nearly one hour. Then a wheel came off and he had to spend another hour fixing it. Old Padhihari stood nearby, watching from under a tree, grumbling all the while. 'Why are you taking so much time, Rajula? The old fool has become useless. Why don't you give up this work if you can't do it?'

Rajula did not seem to mind Padihari's taunts. He continued his work, a smile hovering on his lips. The cow's head lolled lifelessly. Its eyes were open. Its legs, bound together, pointed in the direction of the sky. The end of the tail dangled near one of the wheels. A few large flies fluttered merrily around the body. A group of ants also crawled all over it. It was impossible to know if they were as happy as the flies.

It took Rajula half-an-hour to push the trolley out of the backyard of the Padhihari house on to the road. Was it Rajula who pushed the trolley on? Or was it the momentum of the heavy trolley which pulled the old man along?

The Padhihari family was relieved. The unholy thing had finally been taken away from their house. The farmhands washed and cleaned the ground where the cow carcass had lain. Water sanctified with tulsi leaves was sprinkled everywhere. The house had been defiled since the previous night, when the cow had died. After the dead body was removed and holy water applied, it was deemed clean again.

The day the cow had been brought to the Padhihari household, Padhihari's grandchildren had demanded that she be named 'Kalu'—the black one. Their grandparents had come out bearing a platter with items of ritual worship upon it. They had drawn a long vermilion mark on the animal's forehead and declared that she would be named 'Lalu' and not 'Kalu'. Finally, after lengthy debate and deliberations, everybody had chosen 'Lalu'. A small bell was tied under Lalu's throat. Small pieces of red cloth were wrapped around both her horns and a garland was slid around her neck. Someone had even taken a photograph of the cow with the Padhihari family. The little granddaughter had declared that she would sit on the cow's back and have her photograph taken. Her grandfather had then explained that human beings do not sit on cows, only the gods do. Each body-part of the cow is the seat of some god or goddess. In her mouth, Vishnu, propped up in the posture of eternal sleep, Lakshmi by his side. A thousand-petalled lotus sprouts from Vishnu's navel and Lord Brahma sits in meditation upon it. Rama, Sita, Lakshman and Hanuman are said to travel on cow-back. There is a god on each hair of the cow's tail.

Lalu was therefore a sacred creature. The Padhiharis used to apply a spot of its dung on the foreheads of their children to save them from the evil eye. The courtyard of the Padhihari house was leeped with water and cow-dung to make it holy and germ-free. A whole areca-nut was put on a little ball of dung and placed on the platform where the holy basil grew. This was worshipped as Lord Kuver, the God of wealth. That was the kind of position Lalu occupied when she was alive. But the sacred creature had breathed her last at about eight the previous evening. Lalu was a milch cow with two grown-up calves. The Padhiharis used to get eight litres of milk from her every day. On Raksha Bandhan, she would be pampered with a special diet; then, the entire family would stroke her head and bow before her. Every day, Lalu was given a bath with Dettol and water. An electric fan had been installed in her shed to keep the place cool. Lalu had been treated with care and considered sacred but the previous evening the veterinarian had pronounced Lalu dead at least half-an-hour before his arrival.

The news shocked the old Padhihari couple and tears rolled down their cheeks. They could not eat or sleep that night. Then Rajula Dip had to be called to get rid of the carcass. The moment the cow breathed its last, all the three hundred and thirty million gods who resided in her body left instantly for Heaven, soaring above the Himalayan mountain range at the speed of light, at three hundred thousand kilometres per second. Lalu had become unholy and untouchable after the gods abandoned her body and an untouchable had to be called in to carry it away. The gods never choose bodies of animals like dogs, cats or pigs as their dwelling place. The earth is full of creatures like rabbits, cats, parrots, pigeons, hens and ducks, but the gods prefer none of these animals as their place of repose. Perhaps Lalu's body, covered with tiny fur, was cosier and more comfortable. Besides, the gods received strength from her milk. The panchamrit—curd, honey, ghee and jaggery mixed in milk—which is believed to have a holy and sanctifying effect, and is as good as other milk products, were prepared from Lalu's milk because the gods were believed to reside in her body. But Lalu had now left the world and had thereby transgressed the thin line which keeps the holy and the unholy apart and, in that very moment of transgression, all the gods had left.

Rajula trudged on, pushing the trolley before him. It

would be more correct to say that the trolley dragged the old man on. Rajula stopped a number of times to rest and to drink water. He lurched along the road, pushing the trolley with all the strength he could muster. It was afternoon when he finally saw his own house and he heaved a deep sigh of relief when he reached the front yard. At that very instant the base of the trolley gave way and it broke into two pieces. The carcass slid off on to the front yard; Rajula, too, lay sprawled beside the cow, face up.

He had managed to drag the carcass, ten times his own body-weight, over such a long distance. But there was no smile on his lips. His eyes were dull and no longer reflected their customary child-like glint. Rajula closed his eyes and began to dream—he dreamt of his dead wife.

Many years ago, he and Rajani Rani had planned to buy a new trolley-cart. But the plan had not materialized for want of two hundred rupees. Rajani had given Rajula a verbal account of her earnings. Twenty rupees from the police inspector, ten rupees from Buthi-master, ten rupees from the havildar's house, another ten from the writer's house, fifteen rupees from the house of the Thakurs, forty rupees from the R.I. Office, ten rupees from the Pathan family, forty rupees at the rate of ten rupees each from the houses of the four hospital nurses, ten rupees from the Ghasis, thirty rupees from the Marwari family and the last ten rupees from a Bengali family—a total of two hundred and five rupees—money earned for cleaning human shit. Sometimes she would receive a bonus in the form of leftovers like roti or rice, a little pickle or an onion. If there was a marriage ceremony, Rajani would receive a lot of left-over rice. Even in those days, they could not save enough to fulfill their dream of buying a new trolley. Rajani Rani grew old—she suffered from rheumatism and became bed-ridden. She remained confined to her bed for a year and died. The dream of a new trolley died with her.

Rajula had planned to carry Rajani's body on his trolley-cart and cast it away somewhere. But two fellows from his own caste who lived in a distant village had come to visit on hearing of Rajani Rani's death. They dug a large grave, placed Rajani Rani in it and covered her with earth. Rajula placed a large stone upon the grave. Sitting alone by his wife's grave, he shed silent tears for a long time.

Were she alive, Rajula thought wistfully, the old woman would have taken care of me.

The dead cow lay in the courtyard, the old man lay beside it. After nearly an hour, the old man sat up. Then he tottered into the house to look for a knife. After searching for a while, he managed to get hold of an old butcher's knife. A man walked into the courtyard. 'I will take the cow-hide,' he declared. 'I will pay you two hundred rupees for it. You get on with cutting and dressing it. Don't sell it to any other fellow—got it?' Rajula nodded. The man went away.

The old man stood for some time, leaning on the door of his hut. He rested his head on the wall. The light in his eyes was fading. His head reeled. The old man closed his eyes and tried to sleep. But he couldn't close them, nor could he dream. He tried to smile but his lips felt stiff. His hands and feet trembled. Clutching at the wall and leaning against it for support, Rajula walked slowly up to the carcass. He bent forward and, with the blunt knife, tried to cut loose the rope which held the animal's legs together. After two or three attempts, the rope began to give way. One of the legs, very stiff by now, came loose and struck the old man's head with great force. He fell on to the carcass. For about a minute or so, his lips trembled and his eyelids fluttered; his nose, fingers and cheeks quivered. Then, everything became still and motionless. Old Rajula had finally become a corpse.

His most cherished possession, his last box of dreams, lay there, abandoned. The thick darkness of the last ninety days had displaced the dream it once nurtured.

Kaniska

THE CAVERN IN which Kaniska reposed, smeared with sleep, blood, breath and flesh—how beautiful it was; an unworldly place almost like heaven. Kaniska lay in slumber in the petal-soft bed of the womb; a fearless, worriless traveller dozing in the shade of a road-side tree, an insect in a tender bud.

But the noises of the earth woke Kaniska and killed him. Kaniska had no power to resist or ignore the crowd of feelings, the jostling of so many words. He had no choice.

So Kaniska slid down to earth, having burst open the walls of his cell. He was an earthen ball released, the lion-headed Vishnu bursting out of a pillar.

The moment he emerged, Kaniska was taken away to be cleaned. Medicines, bandages and cotton-wool were used. Someone, perhaps the nurse, held Kaniska upside down. Kaniska floated in a void—a tortoise swimming in reverse—a well-grown, healthy baby.

After a long time, Kaniska uttered his first cry; like the first showers of monsoon, his cry melted the frozen soul, drove away all fear from the heart, thawed the cold tension building up in the Emergency room and swept clean the dirty spider webs of premonition from the minds of anxiously waiting relatives. It brought a smile to every face.

Kaniska cried as if he was under some intoxicated spell; he cried and cried till the smiles were wiped off everyone's lips. Then the doctors cut the umbilical cord and Kaniska made his entry.

As time passed inexorably, Kaniska began to grow up. He would often be found waving at the sky; he grew up under its tranquil beauty, under its care and in its company. He adopted the sky's demeanour and its calm forbearance.

Then from nowhere, without notice, a storm tiptoed into the calm expanse of Kaniska's sky; it was found that Kaniska had defective eyesight. He could not distinguish objects or identify colours—red petals, red balloons, red blood, red bandages, red lips, all escaped Kaniska's sight. He could not recognize his parents, his doctors, the nurses; he could not even differentiate between the door and the wall. A series of tests were conducted. Many pairs of eyes scanned the insides of his brain and eyes and scrutinized the wild growth of tissues there. Kaniska whimpered and moaned but nobody paid heed. Outside the operating room, many pairs of eyes overflowed with tears and hope. Fortunately, the operation was successful. Kaniska could now recognize colours and differentiate between them. He could see and make distinctions between the sari, the sky, the birds, the lips, the bandages and the green leaves of the banana tree swaying in the breeze.

Just when everything seemed to be falling into place, another heart-breaking discovery was made. Kaniska had no sense of hearing.

He could not hear the tinkling of bangles or the rustle of saris. He could not hear the beating of the heart that surged with explosive emotions, the screams hidden within the open mouth, the long, deep sighs of anguish, the groans of a broken-winged bird—the sound of sacred hymns did not enter his ears.

There seemed to be no end to his misfortune. It was soon discovered that Kaniska had no sense of touch either. Ants bit him, bugs stung him, but Kaniska did not feel any pain.

The ache of gnawing hunger, the pain of a pus-filled wound, the scorching heat, the icy chill—nothing could pierce his skin or his flesh and travel up to his brain. Kaniska could not react or resist.

He was just a mass of flesh, as unresponsive and unfeeling as a lump of clay. He blinked stupidly like a doll.

He stood like a baby Christ nailed to the cross.

He twisted himself like the sage with eight deformities, a child Ashtavakra.

Kaniska was like a Neanderthal baby of the Ice Age. The world was a grey, mute TV screen for him.

For Kaniska, everyone was God. Everyone was his destiny.

~

A young baby sitter arrived from the other side of the mountain to look after Kaniska. She was a girl of twelve. She wore a frock that was torn at the back and looked like the upturned cover page of a picture book. She would kiss the plump, cherubic Kaniska, sit him on her lap and sing him lullabies. She would brush his teeth, wash his face and powder him. She would carry him to the garden and show him butterflies, she would show him the moon and the mirror. She would try to protect him from danger— she would keep him away from glass bottles, from the garbage heap and from stray dogs. She would prevent Kaniska from running into walls and other obstacles and hurting himself. She became Kaniska's destiny, his saviour, his armour in the uneven battle of life which he constantly fought. Sometimes, Kaniska would clutch her tightly. He was remarkably strong. The young girl would tremble—she was afraid of Kaniska's strength.

At times Kaniska bit her and drew blood; then she would cry uncontrollably. She would beg her master and mistress to send for her father who would take her back to her village. She would repeat that demand the entire evening. But by the following morning, she would have forgotten everything; all her complaints would have become a thing of the past. She would place

Kaniska on her lap and kiss him, she would take him to the bathroom, undress him and bathe him. She would laugh playfully as she soaped him. She would laugh till she was out of breath. She would touch the absurd, fleshy toy which dangled from his body. She would pour water on him, rub the dirt off his body, and play with his fleshy toy. She would laugh uncontrollably as a strange excitement would sweep over her. Kaniska would gaze at her innocently, his face expressionless. His eyes would hold a vacant look. He did not understand the cruel jokes of destiny.

Filling in empty spaces was a matter of habit for Kaniska. He would open his mouth and insert his finger into it. He would poke his chubby fingers into small holes in a wall. He would pour sand and water into any hole that he came across. He would put his fingers into his father's nostrils and his mother's ears. Sometimes, he would even poke the poor babysitter in her eyes.

It is an ancient habit of man to fill up empty spaces; he has always been preoccupied with filling up empty wombs and empty tombs.

Kaniska could utter only vowel sounds but the young babysitter was an expert in ascribing meaning to that gibberish.

If Kaniska said 'Ah', she would, on different occasions, explain that he wanted rice, bread or milk.

If he said 'Eh', she would interpret it as an expression of his desire to have the babysitter powder him, change his clothes, kiss him, and chase butterflies.

Kaniska's 'Uh' would mean he had seen some insect or a mouse or a wound or blood.

And when Kaniska said 'Oh', the babysitter would conclude that he wanted to play with Tommy the dog, or the calf or to browse through his picture book.

Whenever there was a mela in town, the babysitter would be asked to escort Kaniska there. At the fair grounds, Kaniska would see the milling crowd of grotesque-looking scarecrows. They would be clad in oddly colourful, tattered clothes, perhaps worn for Holi. Their faces, to Kaniska, looked like inverted, blackened earthen pots on which shapeless eyes had been marked out with lime. They wore bushy moustaches over their thick ugly lips; their hands, feet and fingers were made out of hay. Some of them carried placards with meaningless, raucous slogans.

There were birds inside the mela tent which fluttered their feathers in distress and despair. They seemed to be trapped in that colourful, canopied confinement. There was no sky where they could take flight, no opening through which they could soar up to such a great height that they might take the dotted patches on earth for grains.

Kaniska's eyes would slide off the scarecrows and the terrified, trapped birds and centre on the taxidermied ladies in the houses, on the porches, at the windows along the corridors and on the balconies. The women would flaunt their artificially stuffed body parts; their wide, made-up eyes; their gorgeous saris with sharp-edged borders; their red lips like bombshells; their voluptuous bosoms, insolent and pointed like bayonets. The whole town looked like an absurd show to Kaniska, a bizarre pageant of arrogant, made-up women and ugly, repulsive scarecrows.

Kaniska curled his lips in disgust, made faces, and watched the activities in the bazaar with indifference. The young babysitter stumbled and clutched Kaniska even more tightly. Many a reptile crawled over her budding, youthful body as she did so.

After Kaniska's parents left for work, the babysitter would be left alone with the boy for the entire afternoon. She would draw a circle and place him at its centre, a love angel in an infinite space, striving to fill it with meaning; she would also put her most cherished possessions within the circle: her dreams, a mirror, her wet lips, her gleaming eyes, her black, sleek hair, and above all, the chubby Kaniska. He was *her's*, she would tell herself proudly. She would sprout fresh green wings and flutter all around him. She would deck Kaniska and herself up with wild flowers; she would contort her face and tease her own image in the mirror. Her lips would curl into a small, mischievous smile. She would kiss the mirror and the boy. She would then powder Kaniska and also apply powder to her image in the mirror. She would put a bindi on Kaniska's forehead and do the same to her reflection in the mirror. She would fix the end of her sari on her shoulder with a safety pin and adjust it over her chest. Then she would examine herself in the mirror.

Sometimes, she would deliberately let the sari slip off her bosom, revealing her youth, look at herself and wonder if the mirror had captured her secret act of mischief.

She would also make crowns out of newspapers and place them on Kaniska's head. She would fashion garlands out of flowers and put them around the boy's neck. She would colour her own hands and feet with mehndi and lac-dye and play games with Kaniska.

With the setting of the sun, her life would cease to be a game. The world of dreams would recede and the harsh realities of life would come rushing in, as if they had been waiting eagerly in the wings all along. With dusk would float in the images of the scaffold, the burning pyre and of life groaning upon them.

Finally, one day, her father arrived with a bullock-cart to take her away. She was no more a little girl; she was now a young woman and would have to return home across the mountain. She would have to go back to where she had come from several years ago.

She refused. She wept inconsolably. 'Go away. I will not come with you,' she shouted between angry sobs.

Her father laughed at her. Others tried to placate her. 'You have to go back some day or the other,' they said. 'One day, you have to return where you came from, marry a nice man and make your own home,' they urged. 'This is the way of the world. Why do you weep, silly girl?' But the girl declared that she would never leave Kaniska. She would marry Kaniska and no one else—they would play hide-and-seek all day long. They would make a home of their own—a home brimming over with sounds of laughter, games and happiness! They would flutter around it like colourful butterflies. The girl continued to weep but no one took her seriously.

She was sent off with many gifts. There was rice, vegetables and coconuts. There were even clothes for the girl and her father. She was also given a cash gift of five hundred rupees. All the gifts were loaded on to the bullock-cart.

Choking on her sobs, the young girl touched everybody's feet. She hugged Kaniska tightly and held him so close to her that he almost became breathless. She touched his soft palms to her lips. She wept oceans of tears. Her neck was like a thirsty handkerchief which soaked up the rivers of tears flowing from her eyes.

She climbed on to the bullock-cart, lay down on the bed of straw and never woke up.

The bullock-cart trundled away. It grew smaller and smaller and finally disappeared into the horizon like a dream or a mirage. Here, Kaniska was busy chasing butterflies, a stone in hand. He did not understand the goodbyes, the tears and the agony of separation.

The orange western sky where the sun stood witness to all this looked like an expansive canvas on which some great artist had just completed a masterpiece in oil.

For a tiny fraction of a second a serene smile seemed to light up Kaniska's eyes as he gazed afer the disappearing cart.

A Letter from Mesopotamia

THE LETTER ARRIVED when it was least expected. It was addressed to my uncle, my father's elder brother. It came from a place he had heard of, and the strangest thing about it was that my father had actually written it!

By that time everyone—except, of course, my mother—had lost hope that my soldier father was alive. She kept wearing bangles as well as the vermilion spot on her forehead. A year earlier, a rumour had spread that Father had committed suicide and all our relatives had forced Mother to live a widow's life. They perpetrated all kinds of torture—both physical and mental—upon her when she disobeyed them. She did not protest, nor did she try to convince people that her husband was alive, but ignored their abuses with calm defiance. She did give up eating non-vegetarian food, though. Her stubborn denial brought tremendous censure upon her, as well as many deploring and damning adjectives. Some called her a wilful woman while others went to the extent of calling her a slut. People openly described her as my uncle's mistress. But nothing could persuade her to change her mind. She drank the venom of all aspersions and swallowed a flood of silent tears with stoic resignation.

The letter was irrefutable evidence of her unshakeable trust in her own instincts. It put everyone else in the dock.

The letter bore the stamp of an alien place which almost no one in our family had ever heard of.

> I am writing from Gallipoli, from a Mesopotamian ship. We lost the battle in Gallipoli but won in Basra and Amra. We fought there for two long months. It is unbearably hot here. There is not enough water to drink; many soldiers have fallen victim to heat and hunger, and to malaria; to say nothing of the ones who lost their lives on the battlefield. Just ten of us have survived by some miracle. And we are coming back in this ship. How is Shakuntala? I had taken the bicycle belonging to the Maharaja to Sambalpur six years ago. The police had recovered it and kept it in the police station there. Did the Maharaja get his bicycle back? The ship is anchored in Gallipoli. We will start the journey after a week.

My uncle and others had vague knowledge of a war being fought somewhere, but none of them had any idea about Mesopotamia or Gallipoli, Basra or Amra. For nearly one month they remained in the dark. In the end my uncles enquired of a British sahib and learned that Mesopotamia was a far-off land to the west of India. The World War was still raging. But the British army had lost in Mesopotamia and some Indian soldiers were being sent back. Janardan Panda, my father, too was coming back. The news spread like wildfire to the neighbouring towns. All our relatives—uncles, aunts and cousins on both the paternal and maternal sides—came to know about it in no time.

~

My father had married my mother when she was a child. After seven years of marriage, my mother, then fifteen, was sent off to her in-laws' house after the customary rituals were observed. A short time later, my father brought her along to where he had been posted. My father worked in the police department. Sturdily built, tall and possessed of muscular arms and incredible courage, my father looked every inch a man of law. His office provided him with a horse to carry letters from one place to another. He received a total monthly emolument of three rupees—two rupees as salary and one for the horse's maintenance and care. He was allotted a one-room accommodation in the police lane. He used to carry my mother on horseback with him at times, mostly when travelling from Bolangir to Patnagarh or to Titlagarh—relatively long distances. My mother's feeble protests would never work once he made up his mind. He would lift her and place her on horseback with a triumphant smile. A lash from his whip and the animal would gallop off. Everybody, including wild animals, would timidly give way to them. Women would gape at them through chinks in door panels and men would watch goggle-eyed as they stormed through villages and towns. 'Look at the royal couple riding off,' they would say to one another. When they would return after a few days, my mother would invariably be wearing garlands, and baskets of fruits and vegetables would be loaded on horseback. 'The flower lady,' people would remark in amazement. My mother would never smile at the compliments but my father would—a rambunctious, arrogant smile which had a predatory quality about it.

Once when they returned from Titlagarh, a dead deer was slung on horseback along with the inevitable baskets of fruits, flowers and vegetables. People watched on in awed silence. That night, delicious deer-meat curry was cooked in every house in the police lane. Later, people came to know that my father had lunged at the deer from horseback quick as lightning and clamped its neck with his strong fingers. The poor animal had had no chance. Panic made my mother lose her balance as my father jumped off the horse and she fell down, bruising and scratching herself all over. She never went out with my father after that. In those three years, my mother accompanied my father when he travelled on official work only six times. And every time she did, a fine of four annas was deducted from my father's salary. But Father cared little for that. Nor did he care for the admonishments and warnings of his superiors. And he would laugh away the advice and caution of his friends and neighbours.

There were rumours that Father would lunge not only at the deer in the jungle but also the young tribal women he would meet there. There was always a smile of savage delight on his face when he galloped home.

There is an interesting anecdote about Father's daring. He was once on his way to Patnagarh when he came across a man wearing a prisoner's uniform. The man had wrapped a cloth around his left ankle to conceal the metal shackle. The man's suspicious movements raised my father's doubts. He called out to the man and asked him where he had got the uniform from. The man did not say anything and tried to run away into the jungle. My father took a flying leap at the man from his speeding horse and both of them came crashing to the ground. My father effortlessly pinned the man flat on the ground and punched his face bloody. He then slung the man— by now unconscious—onto horseback and sped to the police station. A big crowd had gathered there. The man my father had captured was a murder convict who had been sent to jail two months earlier. He had broken out of prison only a few days ago.

Stories about my father's brawn and his bravery spread to the surrounding towns and villages after this incident. The capture of the convict was even registered in the records of the government. Eventually, the tale travelled to the Maharaja. My father received clothes and a pair of shoes for his gallantry. It was the first pair of shoes my father had ever possessed in his life. He wore them everywhere. The sound which the shoes made as he strode around in them would fill my father with an overwhelming sense of pride and satisfaction. At times, however, he would tie them with a length of rope and carry them on horseback.

The Maharaja had got three Raleigh bicycles from Calcutta to gift to some of his efficient officials. On learning about Father's adventure with the convict, the Maharaja invited him to his palace and gifted him one bicycle as a token of appreciation. The Maharaja also assigned Father the job of delivering the royal post. Father, thereafter, rode the bicycle as well as the horse as it suited him. And as before, the menfolk would stand on the roadside watching in amazement while the women would peep through half-opened doors as my father rode past.

~

Gambling was my father's obsession. He used to stay away from home for days and return carrying valuable jewellery. But the sight of that jewellery glittering brilliantly in the sunlight never brought a sparkle of excitement to my mother's eyes. Father used to put the ornaments into an earthenware pot, lid it, and then wind a piece of cloth tightly around the pot. But usually, in less than a week, the ornaments would disappear as mysteriously as they had come. The shards of the pot were proof that Father had lost the jewellery gambling. This had become routine in our family. That was perhaps why the dazzle of the ornaments never reached my mother's eyes. Whenever Father would win money, he would buy nearly half the stock available at the sweetmeats shop in town and distribute it among our neighbours. The day he won a goat, almost the entire neighbourhood would eat mutton curry. Everyone would celebrate with Father, wish him luck, and pray that his winning spree would never end.

Then there was that episode when Father stole my grandparents' money and valuables. Father was bankrupt and badly needed money. Finding no other way to cover his loss, he went to my mother's parental home and lifted some ornaments and other valuables. Soon the truth came to light and Father, genuinely repentant for the shameful way he had acted, went to Sagarpalli and lay prostrate on the ground clutching at my grandfather's feet. He wouldn't leave my grandfather's feet, my father vowed, until he was forgiven. He lay there in the dusty foreyard in the burning heat of the sun. My grandfather, angry and adamant, refused to give in to my father's entreaties. For nearly one hour people—standing in shade—watched on curiously. My grandmother brought them some water to drink. Neither the old man nor his son-in-law budged. My grandmother brought a couple of wet cloths and placed one on the old man's head and the other on my father's. Both of them flung the cloths away. Another hour passed, and then one more. At two in the afternoon, finally, my grandfather asked my father to get up. 'Okay okay,' he said, 'I forgive you. Now get up.' To my grandmother he said, 'Let's eat. Lay out the food.' They all came into the house and the crowd slowly dispersed.

~

Maharaja Prithviraj Singhdeo loved a life of luxury and spent lavishly on rejoicing and revelry.

Once, he invited some gamblers to his palace. The winner, he announced, would be adequately rewarded. The event continued non-stop for three days. The Maharaja, seated comfortably in a huge, heavily cushioned chair, watched the game with great interest. His boisterous laughter and loud encouragements filled the atmosphere with a cheery liveliness. The gamblers had the rare fortune of enjoying a meal of sweetened rice and delicious meat curry cooked specially for the Maharaja. The food was served in bone china and drinks in silver glasses. It was like living in a kind of paradise. It was the realization of a long-nurtured dream for Father and his gambler friends. So overwhelming was the experience that it blunted the edge of even the biggest loser's frustration. Putting all at stake and losing everything did not prick him in the least. Quite the opposite, insolvency brought him bliss. My father won three necklaces, five rings and fifty rupees in that game. The Maharaja gifted him a gold bracelet and an expensive silk shawl.

It was time for celebration. Two goats were slaughtered and the meat distributed among half the people in town. Father had asked the owner of the biggest sweetmeats shop to supply rasgullahs. Everybody who came to our home to see the Maharaja's gifts and the prizes Father had won was offered rasgullahs. Strangely, rejoicing on such grand scale could not bring back the sparkle to my mother's eyes.

My grandfather arrived to congratulate Father and wanted to keep the bracelet and the shawl as a memento of the Maharaja's generosity. Father gave them away happily to him and carried my grandfather back on his bicycle to his village Sagarpalli. 'You have walked miles to reach, I can't let you walk back,' he said. Father rode back all the way from Sagarpalli immediately after leaving Grandfather at home, without stopping anywhere for a rest.

~

There was a woman, a milkmaid, who they said was my father's 'kept'. My father used to gift her jewellery and even provide her financial support. The Brahmin community in our locality disapproved of this relationship. But my father's affluence, his valour, his reputation and political clout prevented them from saying anything openly. Possessed of a strong character, my father openly went against orthodoxy. He did not care to wear the sacred thread of the Brahmins but wore a moustache instead.

He ate eggs and chicken, and did not conform to religious regulations. He rode horses, wore leather shoes and belt, and gambled and womanized. The senior and more important members of the Brahmin community found it terribly humiliating to put up with my father and his wild ways.

They ganged up and planned to catch my father red-handed in the company of the milkmaid. They had to wait for a month for the right opportunity. They surrounded her house one midnight and broke into it. 'Where is Janardan?' they charged. They abused and thrashed the milkmaid but could not tell them where my father was. The Brahmins looked for my father through the night but could not find him. They even came to our house. My mother, utterly confounded by these developments, passed into a state of a shocked silence for a couple of days. There was no trace of Father; it was as if he had disappeared into thin air.

It was only when, after six long years, Father wrote the letter from Mesopotamia that everyone came to know what had happened on that fateful night. Actually, Father had fled Bolangir for Sambalpur that very night on his bicycle. In Sambalpur he sold the bicycle for fifty rupees. Later, the person who bought the bicycle was interrogated by the police; they wanted to know where he had got the special Raleigh cycle which the Maharaja himself had ordered from Calcutta. On learning the facts, the police sent for my father. My father did not come to the police station. Instead, he punched the man who had come to fetch him. The man collapsed. Some onlookers rushed to his aid. They sprinkled water on the man's face and tried to bring him back to consciousness. My father took the chance and fled.

He boarded a Calcutta-bound train and, on reaching, got himself drafted into the British Army. This was during the First World War and the British government was in dire need of soldiers. Soon after he joined the British Army, Father was sent to Mesopotamia.

My mother stayed for nearly six months in her in-laws' house. Then for the following two years she lived with her mother in Brahmapura. After the death of my uncle's wife, Mother stayed in his house with her own daughter and took care of his four young sons. She accompanied him to the places where he was transferred. I was not born at that time. People called her my uncle's mistress and looked upon her with contempt and censure.

Father returned to his native land after six years.

~

On reaching Calcutta he wrote again to his elder brother and wanted to know what had happened to the bicycle-theft case against him. My uncle made inquiries and learnt that the case did not exist anymore. In the two months that he stayed in Calcutta Father suffered from malaria and his money and belongings were stolen. A man of broken health and virtually reduced to a pauper,

Father had no choice but to request his elder brother to take him back. It took about fifteen days for my uncle to make the necessary arrangements and, finally, my father came to Kantabanji with him. He stayed for a couple of months in Kantabanji and moved to Titlagarh to work for a rich businessman there.

Khusiram Jain, the man my father worked for, was in the money-lending business. He was greatly impressed with my father's well-built, robust figure and his reputation as an ex-armyman and engaged him in the job of collecting interest from his debtors. Due to his imposing presence, my father had no problem with any debtor. He was provided with accommodation in Titlagarh and a bicycle as well so that he could travel to distant villages to collect money. A few months after he started working for Jain, father brought his wife and daughter to Titlagarh. There they lived a life of peace for about three years. It was during his stay at Titlagarh that I was born. But my family was not destined to enjoy that peace for long.

Khusiram Jain, my father's employer, was a cruel and greedy man—even though he never let that side of his character surface when dealing with my father. But he had created a number of enemies because of his harsh and rude manners. One winter night, Khusiram was supervising the manufacturing of gud—made by boiling sugarcane juice in large cauldrons—when four men killed him. They then cremated his body in the earthen furnace.

By morning the body was so completely burnt that not even a piece of bone could be traced. The previous night, my father had left for a distant village to collect interest due to the moneylender. He learnt about his employer's brutal death only when he returned after four days. For the next two months he was called to the police station time and again and interrogated. But the police was finally convinced that he was not involved in any way in Khusiram's murder and let him go.

Carrying only bare amenities and his wife and children on his bicycle, my father rode to Bangomunda as soon as the police permitted him to leave Titlagarh. He settled there with his family and worked for Sadananda Bhoi, the local zamindar. He was assigned the job of tax and revenue collection. My brother, the youngest of us all, was born during our stay in Bangomunda. Father, in the meanwhile, had fallen into bad company and was becoming involved in all sorts of skirmishes and brawls with the village folk. He made enemies in the Brahmin community because of his impudence and nonconformist nature. He was often seen with drug-takers and the other riff-raff of the village. He became friendly with Alekh Padhihari, a distantly related uncle, and developed the habit of taking opium. Because he had joined the British Army, father was declared an outcaste and despite repeated reminders never bothered to perform the prescribed rituals which would readmit him into the community.

Six years passed. And then, suddenly, without suffering from any significant ailment, Father died. He was only fifty.

It was six o'clock in the morning when he breathed his last. We were excommunicated and no one from the Brahmin community came forward to assist us in the funeral arrangements. People belonging to the other castes could not volunteer any help for fear of antagonizing the Brahmins. It was not possible to wait for our uncles to arrive after receiving the news—that would take days. Our neighbours advised that we should carry Father's body on a cart to the cremation ground. In the beginning nobody was prepared to lend his cart but someone finally consented to let us use his cart, in exchange for Father's bicycle. It required exceptional effort to haul the body up on to the cart. My sister was thirteen at that time, I was six and our youngest brother was a just a toddler. Mother and my sister held the body on its head-side. I dragged both the legs and after labouring for nearly an hour or so we managed to load the body on to the cart. The zamindar sent a length of white cloth to be used as a shroud. My mother and sister pulled at the yoke of the cart and dragged it along the uneven track for nearly half a mile. At last we arrived near the cremation ground and stood the cart under a tall, spreading tree. We lifted the wheel on one side and tilted the cart so that the body would roll over on to the ground. We covered the body once again. We went searching for a hole nearby that would hold the body and, finding one, we dragged the body there and rolled it into the hole. After covering the hole with earth and some branches and twigs we walked to a pond and bathed. We wept all the way home.

That day, Mother ate nothing. The day following was the eleventh day of the moon's fortnightly phase, and it was customary for a Hindu widow to keep a fast on that day.Mother ate nothing on that day too. She did not even drink a drop of water. Some goodhearted neighbours sent food for us and the three of us managed with that.

We performed the funeral rites following the advice and guidance of some well-wishers and neighbours. We had to sell utensils and whatever little valuables were left with us to meet the expenses. My elder uncle arrived on the ninth day and stayed with us for two days. The journey and spending two days with us had cost him three rupees, he complained before he left. Months later, my maternal uncle and my father's two younger brothers paid a short courtesy visit. They had brought some biscuit packets, fruits and vegetables. We somehow managed to sustain ourselves on the charity of our neighbours and village folk for another month or two.

Then somebody suggested to my mother that she go begging. She had no choice left. One morning she went out to seek alms, veiling her face and carrying my kid brother in her arms. She stood at the doorstep of a rich Marwari businessman's house and wept. The Marwari family took pity on her and gave her a generous quantity of food. They also gave her some money. The food and money lasted us nearly two days. Then mother picked out one rich Marwari family after another in the vicinity. Slowly, begging became a habit and she no longer felt any discomfort. Begging, fortunately, turned out to be a rather easy alternative to waging difficult struggles for survival. Every morning she would go out carrying her little son in her arms and return after four or five hours, her bowl filled with rice and different varieties of pulses and other eatables. There was money, too. We no longer remained hungry. Mother used to give us a little opium at night and we would enjoy a sound, restful sleep. In a way begging made our life comfortable.

~

That day, Mother came back with quite a large quantity of rice and other things. We were very happy and laughed and jested with one another.

'How come none of us has a name?' my sister asked. 'Let's choose a name for every one of us now.'

'All right,' Mother said. 'I would like to name you after the three strange places your father visited abroad. That will be one way to remember him. You will henceforward be Gallipoli Panda. The name of my elder son will be Basra Panda, and the younger one will be called Amra Panda.' Mother laughed happily at her own joke. We too laughed and agreed to our names.

'What about you?' my sister jested. 'I think you should change your name from Shakuntala to Mesopotamia Panda.'

Mother burst out laughing.

Filling in the Blanks

A VIRGIN GIRL of twelve was running across vast cornfields. Narrow ridges separated one farm from another and crisscrossed the barren fields. On the ridges grew weeds and brambles; the tracks were covered with cobbles and stones. With no rain, the land had turned arid and had cracked in many places. The girl ran like a doe being chased by a hunter.

She was dark—her complexion was that of evening giving way to night. She wore red trousers below her navel. There were dark stains of dried blood on the trousers and on the portion of her body above the navel. Her belly, soaked in sweat, heaved as she ran. She wore a sky-blue blouse over the tiny bulges of her breasts. A solitary safety-pin somehow managed to hold the blouse in place. The blouse was torn at the neck. Both the lapels were curled inwards and looked like the torn, dog-eared pages of a child's picture-book. A dirty, white handkerchief was tied around her neck. A tiny pigtail at the back of her head danced this way and that as she sped over the narrow track. Her hair, which looked as if it had not been oiled for days, was dry and lustreless. There were two small punctures on her ear-lobes but she did not wear earrings; instead, a pair of tiny sticks stoppered the holes. From the faint stains on her toenails, it seemed she had applied lac-dye to her feet several days ago. The girl ran desperately, as if her very life depended on it. She looked very frightened. A small bird flew overhead; perhaps it had escaped a cage, perhaps that was why it flapped its wings so hard.

A cage is like a blank space. Every moment of our existence, we play the game of filling in such blank spaces. We spend a lifetime trying to fill in the blank spaces of our lives—the effort wears us out and leaves us with little to show at the end of the day. The spaces remain blank. Yet it is not in our hands to stop the game, nor can we resist playing it even though it is destined to end in our defeat. All our efforts, expertise and competence fail miserably.

How spontaneously does a baby insert his thumb into his mouth and fill that blank space.

The emptiness of the heavens can easily be filled in by assigning God residence.

The emptiness of space can be filled with a satellite.

The empty womb with seed.

The empty tomb with a corpse.

The empty pyramid with a coffin.

The empty desert with pyramids.

The game of planting words on the blank pages of a newspaper can be played on and on, for ever.

The game of filling in the blank spaces on the hit-list of a terrorist group.

The game of filling an empty gun with bullets.

The game of razing a city to the ground with a bulldozer.

Adult human beings keep playing the game of filling in blanks without pause, without scruple, without shame.

Yet, at times, someone's vacant eyes have to be filled with dreams, a bird has to be put into the empty space under someone's ribcage; all consolations and promises in love letters have to be ground, made liquid, and poured down someone's feeding tube; all faith and all gods have to be pushed into the hole under the husking-pedal and pounded into fine dust.

~

The girl sprinted along the track. She trampled thorny shrubs, cut her feet on cobblestones, and raced over dry, cracked land. Her strength was draining but she did not stop, she bounded on like a frightened doe.

It was a wide panorama stretched over a massive canvas: a single figure of the little girl drawn against the vast backdrop of the arid land. Now, another figure stepped into the panorama from behind a dense growth of trees. It was the figure of a massively built, muscular man. He wore a turban, grasped a staff in one hand and a funnel-shaped blow-horn in the other. His eyes were bloodshot, like a ferocious tiger's. He did not run but his eyes raced across the expanse of the meadows and farmlands to the distant skyline. The pupils of his large, round eyes quivered so frightfully fast that it seemed as if they would burn anyone who dared meet them. Faced with this savage force, the little girl would have simply no chance.

The sun shone brightly overhead. The loincloth wound round the man's waist came down to his knees. It was wet with sweat at the waist-line. So, too, was the man's naked torso. Rivulets of sweat trickled down from under his turban and ran along his face and body. Fortunately, the man had not seen the girl. The girl stumbled, fell, and hurt her foot. She smeared a little earth on the bleeding wound and crawled like a lizard into a thicket on one side of the narrow track. She peered fearfully at her pursuer.

The man strode with an air of decisive arrogance; he looked ready to pounce upon his prey.

He planted each step with such great force that it made a deep impression even on the dry, hard earth. Within every impression lay a butterfly crushed to death. The man had no idea that he had squashed so many butterflies under his feet. He marched on; bold, impassive, unperturbed. Did those impressions which his feet made remind one of the footprints of Lakshmi that one paints with rice-paste in the front yard of one's house in the month of Margashir? No, there was nothing holy about those footprints. This was a strange festival—ugly, unholy, savage!

The footsteps went past fields and barns, over hills and through brooks, over depressions and heights, past water canals and streams, over tracks strewn with dead leaves, and finally stopped near a car that was parked on the outskirts of a village. The footsteps took a U-turn and stopped again. Such cars would visit small, nameless villages like this one every once in a while. Those who came by that car would usually bring food for the villagers who had managed to survive; they would advise them to share the food among themselves judiciously. Sometimes, the car would bring them clothes and handkerchiefs; sometimes, they would bring colourful papers which carried printed words and pictures. 'These papers carry hope, solace and promises. They will teach you to dream again, this paper is your passport to safety and security. Fix it to the trunk of a tall tree. Remember, the tree must be strong and not like the wreckage of your huts. Don't waste or misuse these papers.' The people in the car would drive away after warning the villagers thus.

The villagers who had managed to survive shared the food among themselves, but could not decide what to do with the papers. They could have rolled them to make beedis but they did not have any tobacco; they could have given them to their children to play with but there were no children in the village; they could have thrown them into a pile of cow-dung, but not a single cow or bullock could be found in their village. One or two of the villagers faintly recalled having heard of paper being used to make kites or paper-boats. Some also said they had heard of villages where children would write things on paper. 'Paper is meant for the use of children' was the conclusion the villagers arrived at. Hence, it had no use in a place where there were no children, they decided.

The turbaned man walked around the car, staff in hand. He stared at the car wide-eyed; he then squinted and tried to peer in through the glass. But he could see no one and headed towards the village. It was not really a village, just ten or twelve huts with mud walls and a patch of earth littered with the ruins of eight to ten hovels. Several ant-hills had sprung up in the ruins; one could see black insects scurrying about and one or two lizards crawling in the weeds. The tottering huts where people lived had no doors. An empty sack that hung at the entrance served as a door. Each sack-door had several large holes, the holes were covered over by spider-webs and freshly trapped flies.

The man stood in front of one of these huts and called out, 'Dum Budha Majhi!' No one answered. Then, someone coughed inside. The man stood waiting. He saw two gentlemen come out from the other side of the ruined huts. They walked slowly towards him. As they approached, Dum Budha Majhi emerged from behind the sack-door. He had a hand pressed to his chest and held on to the wall with the other. He coughed repeatedly as he stood there unsteadily. One of the gentlemen took out a movie-camera, the other one took out a tape recorder and a small microphone. The big, muscular man came straight to the point. 'Dhania, the granddaughter of Dum Budha Majhi, ran away this morning. No one knows where she's gone.' Casually, he described how he had looked for the girl everywhere but had not been able to find her. His master had ordered him to get the girl back by evening, he said. He repeated what his master had asked him to do in case he failed: 'If you don't find her, go to her grandfather and ask him to return the twenty kilos of kudo rice and the one hundred and fifty rupees he borrowed.'

'Tell me, where is your granddaughter?' the man asked in a threatening tone. Dum Budha Majhi was silent. The news had robbed him of speech, so stunned he was. His head began to spin and he slumped to the ground. He did not hear anything, he did not see anything except the black, blank space in his life that seemed to grow bigger and bigger. He had no one to fill in that expansive, empty space. He had two sons but both of them had gone off to Hyderabad with their wives and children to work in a brick kiln.

They had taken an advance of six thousand rupees from the manager of the kiln. They had nothing left after repaying the loan and paying for travel. It would have been foolish to expect otherwise. Therefore they had kept a little rice and some money for the old man; they had left Dhania behind to give him emotional support, to fill in the void that had been created in the old man's life after his family had gone away, leaving him alone, and merged into the crowd of passengers on the train. Dhania worked as a bonded slave with a moneylender who lived not too far from their hut; the old man and the little girl could at least see each other once in a while. This way, perhaps, they could have managed to survive the loneliness for some more time.

Try as one might, it is not always possible to play the game of filling in the blanks in a systematic, organized way. However neatly you draw your lines, however straight you make them, it becomes difficult to coordinate things. The straight lines tend to get twisted and, if erased, they smudge and blur. When you try to make a fresh start, the lines get tangled into an inextricable mess which make the game impossible to play.

It was explained to Dhania that she would visit her grandfather once in a while; it was also explained to her that she was to be mortgaged to the moneylender for a period of six months. Her parents, brothers and sisters would be back by the end of those six months. She must obey her employer and put up with him until then. It was not even a week and Dhania had already run away. Old Dum Budha Majhi felt as if he had been struck by lightning. Dhania had run away and he would have to return the one hundred and fifty rupees to the moneylender, the money he had hoped would sustain him till his family returned. The turbaned man announced that he would wait until the sun set. Dhania had to return home after dark; where else could she go?

All the old men and women, in the meantime, had gathered near Old Dum Majhi's hut. Everyone held a crutch or a stick, perhaps for support, perhaps for the consolation that there was something to share their burdens of age and agony. Their loose and wrinkled skins were terrifying, sordid maps. It was difficult to find the nose in their old faces—the nostrils, merely two perforations which might have been woodpecker holes in a tree, indicated its presence. Their slightly bulging pupils resembled the small eyes of baby birds which alternately open and shut in the darkness of the nest. Four pairs of dead breasts hung from four old chests like the nests of weaverbirds dangling from a branch, ready to drop off with the slightest breeze. On every old head was a mop of rough, unkempt hair—a tangle of wild bushes. The group of old men and women stood there uncertainly, looking at one another in fear and apprehension. Where would they look for Dhania? Where had she run away? Would she return? Insecurity and doubt tormented everyone. The sun was going down in the west; the light would go out soon, transforming the village into a big, black cavern—great waves of darkness would rush in and drown all the villagers.

That was precisely what happened: no one could guess when and where the car disappeared along with its two passengers in that all-enveloping darkness. The turbaned man continued to sit there, staff in hand—an executioner. Everyone shrank back in fear. Silence invaded the minds of all the villagers, hammered their thoughts with a large stone, crushed them and made them bleed. It was impossible to see one another in that impenetrable darkness even if they huddled close together. They tried to derive some satisfaction by touching one another, but each of them was palpably conscious of the unfathomable gap between himself and the one who stood next to him. The terror of some approaching disaster which they couldn't understand kept lashing them through the night. It shattered them mentally and physically.

Time does not visit godforsaken places like this in the form of hours and minutes. It comes in the form of moments—many, many moments throng to decide the different phases of day and night. When compared to the hands of a clock these moments move very slowly, very sluggishly. An hour can pass quite easily but these lazy moments ruthlessly refuse to budge. The moments of that soul-wrenching night had mercilessly slowed down their pace; they seemed determined not to leave.

Yet, those millions of moments rolled by, one reluctant step at a time, as if prodded on by the turbaned man and his staff. Just before dawn, the man was jerked out of his sleep and let out a loud, shrill cry. The others were startled out of their uneasy sleep. They all looked wide-eyed at the line of blood that had zigzagged like a snake's head into the courtyard as if in search of someone. Not knowing where the trail of blood was headed, all the villagers moved out of its way in panic. The red line slithered down to reach old Dum Budha Majhi, and it took no time for him to understand that it was his granddaughter' blood. In a frenzy, the old man touched a speck of blood to his fingertip and licked it. He cried out, loudly, 'Dhania… My Dhanu… Dhani,' and sprang to his feet. He began to follow the blood trail. The darkness was fast thinning, the group of ten old men and women as well as the turbaned man followed Dum Majhi. They came to an abrupt halt and stared at the series of deep impressions formed by heavy footsteps. Inside every imprint lay a number of dead butterflies. The turbaned man bent down to examine them and realized that these were impressions he had made. It had never occurred to him that he had killed so many butterflies. The man slumped to the ground. His feet refused to move.

The others forged on over rugged, uneven ground, taking turns to push aside the tangled growth of wild creepers. The old man was weeping bitterly and calling out to his granddaughter. He angrily shoved away a sympathetic hand which pressed upon his shoulder. The line of blood trailed along the footprints with the dead butterflies in them and into the depths of the forest. Dum Majhi was tired and drained, as were the others; his voice was beginning to falter. Still, the group walked on as though some otherworldly force urged them on. They walked till the sun had climbed a fair way up in the eastern sky. After four hours or so they noticed that the trail of blood had turned away from the footprints and had moved off in a different direction; they could hear someone sobbing—the sound seemed to come from far away and grew feebler as it moved on. All the tired old men suddenly seemed to come to life.

Forming a semi-circle they groped their way into the jungle. Having searched for some time they finally found the injured and bleeding Dhania squirming behind a thorny hedge. All the villagers broke into tears when they saw her plight. Dhania heard her grandfather calling out her name and opened her eyes. When she found the old man, she hugged him tight and wept bitterly. All the villagers sat near the girl and cried; not one person uttered a word but all of them cried their hearts out. Dhania, too, cried but, above all, relief was the dominant note in her voice—they guessed that she must have escaped savage suffering.

The sight of the dead butterflies had shocked the turbaned man; now, the sight of the bleeding girl and all those old people crying together stunned him even further. Unsure of his role there, he began to slowly back away. But Old Dum Majhi motioned to him to wait.

'My darling child!' He tried to bring conviction into his voice. 'It's just a matter of a few months.' He promised her that she would be back home soon; her parents, too, would return from the city and everything would be all right. She should go back with the man and try to be more understanding. Others reiterated what Dum Majhi said—Dhania must go back to the moneylender;

she would be brought home for the tilling of the fields and the sowing of the seeds. 'Let her go! Let her go!' they chanted.

Dhania protested vehemently. She wailed. How could she go back to that monster? she asked. The other day, the wretch had squeezed her tiny breasts and caused her unbearable pain. It would be suicide to return to that fellow, she declared. Then, all at once, she got up and ran. The turbaned man as well as everyone else followed her into the jungle.

'Dhania! Dhania!' they called after her. Eleven hawks chased after a chicken which had managed to escape them.

The Hunt

SHORTLY AFTER SUNRISE one winter morning, the news that a tiger had killed Hiran Majhi's son, Luchhan Majhi, spread like wild fire through the village of Biripali. Luchhan had taken his cattle to their cornfield on the outskirts of the village. As the cattle were grazing, the tiger stole in and, ignoring the cows, bullocks, goats and sheep, chose Luchhan for its prey. It grabbed him by the throat and dragged him away into the jungle. When the villagers heard the news, they immediately began preparations to hunt the man-eater down. They made a great racket, collected various weapons—axes, hatchets, hoes and scythes—and rushed towards the jungle. Their cows, calves, dogs and cats followed with enthusiasm. The pigeons screeched and fluttered their helpless wings within their cages. How could they guess what had galvanized everyone into action? If by chance their cages had been left open, they too would have fled. The crows and cranes perched on the treetops cawed and cackled at the top of their voices and flapped their wings. The din they created echoed in the skies. It seemed as if not only the villagers but all the animals and birds, too, were getting ready for the hunt. The poor tiger seemed destined to die.

Ten days earlier, the news that a man-eating tiger was on the prowl had spread in Biripali and twenty other villages nearby. Fear lurked in every mind. Human beings of all ages, monkeys and dogs, even birds and insects seemed to be living under the perennial shadow of fear. The farms, the barns, the cornfields and the roads were deserted before evening. Young mothers stopped telling their children fantastic and fearful tiger tales to frighten them to sleep. They had told stories as long as the fear of the tiger was not real. They could do so no longer— the mere mention of the brute would fill them with terror. The news of Luchhan Majhi's death travelled fast; from the village to the town, to the newspapers, to the government and, finally, to the Department of Wildlife. Every morning, shortly after sunrise, fresh rumours would start circulating about the appearance, nature and habits of the tiger, which remained unseen. People talked about the feline: six-feet-long, its gait, the black stripes on its skin, its whiskers, its claws—everything about the tiger was declared special and unique.

'Not everyone can kill a tiger. And a tiger does not usually attack someone who looks straight into its eyes. It only attacks its prey from the rear.' The villagers talked about how the tiger relished human blood; it had already killed seven people. The discussions would go on and on.

They would talk about Rahman, the famous hunter who had come all the way from Assam, and his tiger-hunting techniques. Rahman was said to have killed twenty-two Royal Bengals and ten leopards. He would wear a tiger mask at the back of his head when on a hunt. Rahman's mask bore an uncanny resemblance to his face—big, round eyes and a fierce-looking moustache. But the tiger, the villagers all agreed, was very clever. It never showed up when Rahman was around. Ten rounds of bullets had already been spent in trying to hunt him down. The government had requisitioned one hundred rounds of ammunition and ten more searchlights. Rahman had returned without success, but his father had been sent for. The conversation carried on endlessly and would invariably come back to how the tiger had ripped away lumps of flesh from young Luchhan's neck and abdomen.

~

There were about a hundred of them—both men and women. All of them had run towards the jungle without bothering to look back even once. Some women ran cradling babies in their arms. Children had been warned to stay in the village and not venture out of it at any cost—some stood under a tree, some in a courtyard, terrified. Hiran Majhi and his wife, Jasoda Majhi, were in that jostling crowd, too, wailing and crying, armed with crowbars and axes, all set for an encounter with the man-eater.

When they reached the place where the killing had taken place, a woman held Jasoda back. Jasoda wept loudly; her clothes and hair were dishevelled. She cursed the brute: 'May you fall into some hole and die, you murderer. May you be struck down by leprosy. Let not a single one of your brood survive.' She did not spare the hunters either: 'May the tiger chew you up alive! Have you managed to kill even a single tiger in your lives? I pray to God for your death; may the tiger kill your entire family.' She cursed the sarkar: 'Let this government go to hell. Human life has no value in its eyes. These people will all hide their tails between their legs and vanish when there is a crisis, but they will come right back before the elections and try to lure us with false promises. You spineless creatures!'

Leaving Luchhan's body behind, the villagers rushed into the jungle, raising a cloud of dust. They carried all kinds of tools—hatchets, axes, crowbars, cudgels; some even carried coils of thick rope. Perhaps they planned to capture the tiger, tie it up and drag it along to the village. They spent the next couple of hours searching for the animal, running around here and there, raising a din, and finally failed to do anything of significance except spot a pugmark or two. They then returned, drained and exhausted, to where Luchhan lay.

The murmurs started again. Every other person bragged about what he would have done had they come across the tiger. A man who was wielding a hatchet swore he would have chopped the tiger's tail off. Another declared he would have stoved the tiger's abdomen in with his club. One of them said that he would have broken the tiger's back with one blow of his staff. Then there was the fellow who boasted about how he would have clipped the tiger's whiskers and skinned it alive. Someone else bragged about how he would have tied the tiger up with a rope and dragged it out of its lair.

The lifeless body of the fifteen-year-old Luchhan Majhi lay naked on the ground. The tiger had ripped away lumps of flesh from his neck and abdomen. The corpse was covered in blood. Luchhan's father and the angry villagers stood around the body. The police arrived. The officers of the Wildlife Welfare Department also reached. The investigation began. The officers of the Wildlife Welfare Department measured the pugmarks left behind by the tiger. They also measured the wounds on the body and tried to estimate the size of the tiger's teeth and claws. They tried to reconstruct the attack.

They racked their brains over several interesting questions—which direction had the boy been facing when he was attacked? Had he been standing? Or had he been sitting on the ground? From what distance had the tiger pounced upon him? How was it that the boy had not sensed its presence? How could he have failed to detect the reek of the tiger? In any case, the cattle must have sensed its presence and started running helter-skelter; how was it that the boy had still not managed to save himself? Moreover, why had the boy come all the way to the fringe of the jungle armed with nothing more than a stick? He must have been stupid.

There were long debates and deliberations, arguments and counter-arguments. This went on for all of four hours. Finally, the police and the officials of the Wildlife Welfare Department decided to leave—but they warned the villagers that the body would have to be taken to the city hospital twenty-five kilometres away for a post-mortem.

The sun had already set and darkness was gathering. It was therefore decided that the body would be taken for post-mortem only the following morning. A few of the older villagers were mobilized to guard the body at night. They collected a number of sticks, five lanterns and whatever weapons they could get their hands on at that hour—two swords, two daggers, ten crowbars, a sickle, an axe and a long-handled shovel. To these they added a few hatchets, hoes and four empty tin cans. If a wild animal approached, they would beat the tin cans and frighten it away. They also took along two small battery-powered torches. One of them brought along a pack of playing cards and, another, five measures of peanuts. But they found no opportunity to play cards. They had to spend the entire night beating the cans to keep scavengers at bay. The police jeep, its beacon turned on, made a couple of visits. Some of the men who kept vigil over the body were heavily drunk and beat the tin cans more vigorously than the others. Once or twice, under the influence of alcohol, some of them ran into the darkness of the jungle without any reason and heaped abuse on the tiger. The others had a hard time dragging them back to safety.

In the darkness of the night, the village elders calculated how much it would cost to take the body to the hospital and bring it back after the post-mortem. The jeep-owner would demand at least five hundred rupees. There was no way he could get hold of so much money now, Hiran Majhi said. In the end, it was agreed that every family would contribute five rupees to hire the jeep.

By the time the eastern sky began to turn crimson, the village of Biripali had acquired the look of a busy marketplace. Many people from the neighbouring villages had arrived on their bicycles to catch a glimpse of the body. Anywhere from one hundred and fifty to two hundred curious men and women had gathered. After sunrise, the sheet covering the body was pulled off. There was a near stampede as people jostled each other for a glimpse, handkerchiefs pressed over their noses. The blood had dried and turned black and a swarm of ants and maggots crawled all over the body.

The sun had begun its journey down to the west by the time the money was collected from the villagers and the jeep mobilized. Ten of the villagers went with the body to the hospital. Those who stayed back dug a grave. It was almost midnight when the jeep returned. The body was placed in the grave and covered with earth. It was morning by the time everything was done and the men returned to Biripali.

Hiran Majhi's family observed the funeral rites for the following three days. They shaved their heads, smeared turmeric-water on their bodies and mourned. The women of the family would cover their faces with veils and walk down to the river to take ritual baths. A feast of rice, mutton and country liquor was organized for the villagers. Hiran Majhi's family wore new clothes. Old earthen pots used in the household were thrown away and new ones bought. The floors, the verandah and the courtyards of the house were leeped with cow-dung.

Heated words were exchanged among Hiran's kinsmen. Each of the villagers who had taken the body to the hospital demanded country liquor and one new handkerchief. Hiran Majhi's family fulfilled their demands, too. In this way, amid arguments and counter-arguments, the three days of mourning passed.

Hiran Majhi had to sell off his two milch cows and mortgage his farmland to meet the expenses of the funeral; the whole thing set him back by close to five thousand rupees.

The following afternoon, Jhankar, the old priest, walked four kos to visit Biripali. He walked straight up to Hiran Majhi's house and stood in front of it. A crowd of men, women and children gathered in the village street in no time. Their hearts were beating hard and their faces reflected their curiosity. But they stood silent and motionless. The men huddled together and, almost unconsciously, touched each other's shoulders and arms to make their presence felt. Perhaps they wanted to transmit strength and confidence to others through their touch. The women smoothed back their tousled hair and rolled them into knots at the back of their heads. Some of them tightened or loosened the knots of their saris at the waist and rearranged them over their bodies. The children hid behind their mothers' saris like a hen's brood and watched intently. Men and women of all ages stood waiting, wide-eyed in fear and anticipation.

No one could tell how ancient Jhankar really was; rumour had it that he was more than a hundred years old. He was dark as the night, and short, but his startlingly erect posture gave him an aura of his own. His skin looked smooth and healthy and shone under the combined effect of sweat and the oil with which he massaged his body every day. He sported a silver-haired pigtail topped off with a bel leaf. He had a long vermilion mark on his forehead and a red handkerchief around his neck. He wore a white dhoti around his waist and a pair of talismans made up of tiger claws and consecrated with hymns. Around his left arm he wore four amulets made of seventeen different metals. All kinds of ailments, pain, suffering and sorrow were held imprisoned within those amulets.

Jhankar was accompanied by his two formidable-looking sons, both of whom were more than sixty years old. They carried rice, vegetables, fruits, ghee and clay-lamps. Beside them stood four other men. These four were said to be disciples of the old man. They held water pots, vermilion and flowers. They also wielded an entire repertoire of mantras to appease the gods and goddesses and a great many curses for those who refused to obey them.

They had woken up long before sunrise and, carrying the items for worship, had walked several miles to offer prayers to the eight Chandis in four different temples. After completing the worship they had walked all the way back. There was hunger in their stomachs, a good deal of anger in their minds, and several plans. The villagers who stood in front of them had their heads bowed in awe and respect. How miserable, how helpless and how weak they all appeared before Jhankar and his vicious-looking henchmen. Old Jhankar permitted the villagers to commit all kinds of sins. Anyone who committed a sin could escape retribution with the help of this priest. He drank the sinner's share of venom just as Lord Shiva drank all the poison thrown up by the mythical churning of the ocean. Thus, it was only natural for the villagers to regard Jhankar as their saviour. The villagers were spared the trouble of having to think rationally for themselves and of taking responsibility for their actions. Jhankar saved them from all sorts of worry and they, in return, obeyed him blindly and heeded his advice and warnings. They accepted all his decrees without murmur.

He had assured the cluster of twenty-five-odd villages—Biripali being one of them—that he would always be by their side. Old Jhankar had tamed them, held them under his spell and left them with no option but to obey his command.

Jhankar had a squint and an extraordinarily low-pitched voice. He now began speaking in a register that was just above a whisper. 'Your attention, dear villagers—Hiran Majhi, Jasoda Majhi, Durjan Majhi, Bhaskar Majhi, Aenthu Bhuiya, Agadhu Bhuiya, Leelavati, Parvati, Mahima and others! There is something important I have to tell you. The all-powerful goddess Chandi stands guard over our village, Biripali. How, then, did the tiger dare enter the village? True, it did not venture inside the village proper, but it did reach the outskirts. It came all the way up to Hiran Majhi's field. How? Hiran Majhi's field has its own protective deity, as does everybody else's field in this village. How is it that the tiger did not enter anyone else's cornfield? Not only did the tiger enter Hiran Majhi's field, it even killed his son. Has anything like this ever happened here? Has any tiger dared venture inside our village? Can anyone tell me of one previous instance of a boy from this village falling prey to a tiger? Have you ever heard of anything like this? Why has this happened now? The answer is simple—either Hiran Majhi, or his wife Jasoda, has sinned; they have transgressed the codes of morality and are hiding it from us. They are hiding the truth not only from us but from our mother, goddess

Chandi. That is why this mishap has befallen his family. More incidents such as this will happen; mishaps will strike not just Hiran's family, but all the families of this village. True, he has performed the funeral rites for his son as prescribed by tradition. But that is not enough; the power of the guardian deity of this village has weakened. The goddesses are therefore displeased with you; they are losing their power because people are committing sinful acts in secret. They are not willing to protect the village anymore.

'One single man is responsible for this state of affairs— Hiran Majhi. The village is reaping the consequences of his sin. Hiran Majhi must perform the rituals required to negate the evil effects of his sin. He will have to arrange for a performance of the Naroo Dance in the village on the next full-moon night—there are only seven days left. To pacify the wrath of the goddess of the village he has to offer prayers to her. He has to worship her in his cornfield. Moreover, he has to formally invite the presiding goddess of our village and all of us to attend the ceremony. He will throw a feast for all the villagers on the full-moon day. In addition to all this, there is something else he must do. The tiger has defiled the village. Each and every house must be consecrated with holy water. Hiran Majhi will get a bowl of water, burn incense before it and put flowers in the bowl—he will have to worship the water. Then, he must carry the bowl around the village and sprinkle some water and bow in front of every house in the village. This is the only way to save your village from disaster.'

The old priest stopped and prepared to leave along with his disciples. The crowd immediately made way for them. The villagers heaved a collective sigh of relief. Hiran Majhi and his wife stood paralyzed, as if struck by lightning. The villagers looked at each other, dumbstruck. Their eyes reflected fear and helplessness. Their senses seemed to have been numbed by the dread of the unknown.

The full-moon night was only seven days away. All the arrangements had to be made within the next one or two days. The police jeep visited the village that night; the Forest Department officers, too, drove their jeep to the village. They heard about Old Jhankar's decree from the villagers. Next, it was the tehsildar's turn to visit them the following day. He wanted to hold a meeting with both Old Jhankar and the villagers and try to negotiate a settlement that would suit everyone. But that was not to be. The meeting could not be convened because the old priest did not turn up. No one had any idea what the Naroo Dance meant, or the expenses it would involve.

Finally, the Tehsildar himself went to meet the old priest. On his return to Biripali, the tehsildar explained the ritual of the Naroo Dance to the villagers. 'A man from their village will come here, painted like a tiger. He is the tiger-god; he is believed to carry the tiger's soul within himself. This tiger-god will be ceremoniously welcomed with the beating of drums and cymbals and the blowing of horns; several rituals are to be performed on the occasion. A boy of fourteen from this village—who must belong to the caste of the man impersonating the tiger-god—must fast on that day, wear new clothes and a garland of hibiscus flowers. He will sit in the middle of the road, holding a basket containing offerings and gifts for the tiger-god. But the tiger-god will refuse to accept either the prayers or the gifts offered and insist, instead, that he will devour the boy. The boy will then ask the god for an explanation of his actions. The tiger-god will first abuse the boy's forefathers; he will reveal the facts only later. He will tell the boy that his grandfather had been killed by a tiger and explain that the village had thus been defiled and had to be purified with a performance of the Naroo Dance. This grandfather is still roaming the world, sometimes taking possession of the tiger's restless soul. The tiger goes around killing people, as well as their relatives, who have sinned. After the tiger-god warns the villagers, everyone must fall at his feet, offer him gifts and beg him to forgive them and to accept their prayers. They must bring him money and new clothes; they must promise the tiger-god that they will live unblemished lives. Once the tiger-god accepts your gifts, it means that the villagers are absolved of guilt. No tiger will venture into your village ever again. The goddesses who protect your village will become more powerful after the Naroo Dance. Finally, Hiran Majhi will have to arrange a feast for everybody. This is what Old Jhankar and his disciples demand.'

The tehsildar left after explaining all this to the villagers. In the evening, the villagers drank country liquor and gathered in the courtyard of Hiran Majhi's house. They demanded that Hiran Majhi comply with Jhankar's wishes; they threatened Hiran with dire consequences if he did not follow instructions. Hiran Majhi and his wife wept bitterly and begged the villagers to spare them. They pleaded that they could not afford the Naroo Dance and the rituals associated with it. They could, at best, sacrifice a male goat to the village goddess. They had already organized two feasts; they could not afford another or meet the expenses of the Naroo Dance even if they sold whatever little land they still had left. The tiger had killed their young son. They were left with a daughter who was twelve and who would have to be given away in marriage in a few years. They exhorted the villagers to take pity on them and to understand their hardships, but in vain. The villagers did not budge. Hiran Majhi would be thrown out of the village if he did not organize the Naroo Dance on the next full-moon night, they warned him.

The police jeep patrolled the village again that night. A second jeep also visited. That jeep carried the tiger-hunters. But the villagers saw only the long, bright beam of the searchlight and heard random sounds of gunfire. The following morning some media persons from Doordarshan arrived from the capital and interviewed the elderly and the senior members of the village. They interviewed the old priest, Jhankar, Hiran Majhi and Jasoda Majhi. The old priest and the villagers waxed eloquent on the traditions of their village, spoke at length about the different practices of their clan, explained the Naroo Dance and were very glad. Hiran Majhi spoke about his sorrow and misery. He spoke of the difficulties he had faced in arranging the money to perform his son's funeral rites. He spoke of the help rendered by the villagers, and of their hostility, hatred and exploitation. He spoke of his poverty, his helplessness and his suffering. Jasoda told the journalists how the villagers had conspired to force her to sell their two milch cows and how they had compelled them to mortgage their agricultural land. She complained that some villagers had got drunk the other evening and had abused her in filthy language and threatened to kidnap her daughter. She also complained that the villagers were threatening to excommunicate her family unless Hiran Majhi complied with their demands.

It took four or five hours of hard work on the part of the mediapersons to interview so many individuals. Finally, the interviews were telecast; the villagers watched, glued to the television set. They were excited, some of them were even angry. They were uncomfortable that the entire nation would watch them on TV and hear their voices. The camera had successfully captured their schemes, their superstitions, their deceit and their designs. It was difficult to accept that they had actually said all those things. It was embarrassing to realize that they had given several contradictory statements. The villagers realized it was too late to do anything about it and felt frustrated and helpless.

Hiran and Jasoda, on the other hand, were quite thrilled to see themselves on TV and hear themselves voicing their grievances. 'After this,' Jasoda said, 'it won't matter if we are forced to leave the village, it won't even matter if we die.' But why should we die? she thought defiantly after she returned home. It will either be the villagers, or my family, Jasoda said to herself with determination. Let Old Jhankar do whatever he can, we will never organize the Naroo Dance.

It was night by the time the mediapersons finally left. The village again went to sleep amidst the occasional gunfire and the blaring horn of the Jeep on patrol. Henceforth, the villagers would wake up almost every morning to find bodies of small animals like monkeys, kuliha and hundar strewn about. Some amateur game-hunters were killing innocent animals in the name of tracking the tiger. They usually disappeared from the scene after these killings. The officers of the Forest Department came to the village to make a routine report of the matter to the government. They camped at the nearby inspection bungalow for a few nights but failed to capture the errant huntsmen. The day after, Old Jhankar strode into Biripali. He was seething with anger. He summoned the village elders and the chief to a meeting.

Hiran Majhi, too, was called. Hiran arrived as soon as he received the summons. They demanded of Hiran that he clarify whether or not he would organize the Naroo Dance. Hiran Majhi sat mute, his head lowered. They asked him the same question a number of times but he did not utter a single word. All at once, they saw Jasoda tramping down the road to the meeting place. She walked so fast that halfway down the road, the knot of her sari came loose at the waist and the small coin-box which she kept in her waist-fold fell down. Without betraying an iota of embarrassment, she held her sari in one hand and picked up the box, and perfunctorily wrapped the garment around herself. In that brief moment they glimpsed her bare torso. There were a number of tattoos of various shapes and sizes on her shoulders, arms and breasts. There were figures of snakes, birds and many other creatures and objects. Her hair, tied in a knot at the back of her head, had come loose. Jasoda Majhi quickly fashioned a knot. She waved her hands so violently that her two dozen bangles jingled sharply.

'We are telling you the truth,' she shouted. 'We cannot afford the Naroo Dance, you can do whatever you wish. We cannot obey the orders of Old Jhankar.' Having had her say, Jasoda took her husband by the hand and dragged him back to the house.

That very afternoon, a young girl was seen walking stealthily towards Jasoda's house. She looked around furtively to make sure nobody was watching her. She had wrapped a sari carelessly around her body. The end of the sari trailed along behind her over the dusty road. The upper portion of her body was partially covered. She wore her hair in two small braids. One of them was tied with a red ribbon and decked with a withered flower. She wore bangles on her tattooed wrists; there were tattoos on her calves as well. Her toenails retained the fading stain of lac-dye. Only a few days ago, her cheeks had been round and full, and her eyes had sparkled with laughter. But, in these last seven days, her cheekbones had begun to push through and the laughter in her eyes had died. Had the tiger not killed Luchhan Majhi, he would have married this girl; her name was Sumati Majhi. Sumati entered Jasoda's house. She narrated what Old Jhankar had said after Hiran and Jasoda had left the meeting. She told Jasoda that Hiran's family had been excommunicated from that day onwards.

'You did not comply with Old Jhankar's demands, you refused to organize the Naroo Dance or perform the ritual to purify the village. That is why you are no longer allowed to even step out on to the village streets,' Sumati said. 'You cannot draw water from the common well or bathe in the pond, you cannot cut bamboo from the jungle. You are also barred from buying groceries from Durjan's shop. You cannot work for anybody in the village. You cannot handle an axe or any such instrument, nor can you till your land. You cannot prepare ghee, butter or any other milk product; you cannot ride a bicycle. You cannot even plough.' Sumati went on and on. 'Your family is not allowed into the temple of the goddess, you cannot participate in any village festival. If there is a death in a village, you are not to observe the mourning rites as other villagers do; you cannot speak to anyone in the village, nor is anyone else allowed to speak to you. You will no longer be invited to weddings in the village. Old Jhankar has vowed never to set foot in your house. Anyone who disobeys him will have to pay a fine of two hundred and fifty rupees,' Sumati paused for breath.

Hiran Majhi's twelve-year-old daughter sat by Sumati and wept uncontrollably. Sumati pulled the girl to her and touched her own face to hers. At that moment, Sumati's mother stormed into Jasoda's house. She pulled at her daughter's braids and shouted: 'Come along, you base-born wench, who asked you to come here? Do you want us to pay the fine of two hundred and fifty rupees? The tiger has already killed the man you were to marry, Old Jhankar will destroy you now. Do you want to die, you fool? Come with me.' She dragged her daughter away.

Jasoda Majhi began to wail, 'The tiger has killed you, my dear son. Let the old priest kill the rest of us.'

~

On the day of the full moon, Hiran, Jasoda and their daughter were seen lying in their front yard. They did not have the energy to even stand; they looked shrunken and withered. Their eyes, lifeless and dull, were sunk deep into their sockets; their throats were parched and no sound emerged. A deathly pallor had crept over their bodies and there was no warmth left in them. The parrot had died inside its cage the day before; the plants that they had grown with so much care and love in the courtyard, too, had withered away. Only a grain or two of rice remained stuck to the bottom of the earthen pot; it was full of dirt and cobwebs, peanut shells and blighted grains of rice. Empty tin cans and pots were scattered on the floor of the house, making it ugly and repulsive. The picture of the goddess, pasted on the earthen wall decorated with rice-paste patterns, was torn down the middle. The torn half of the picture, folded obliquely, dangled precariously from the wall. Not much of the goddess could be seen except her upraised hand adorned with gold bangles. The rats had gnawed the cloth-mattress and turned it to tatters. Neither Hiran Majhi nor his wife or daughter could see or hear anything. The light in their eyes had died. Swarms of buzzing flies circled over the foamy saliva flowing out of the corner of the girl's mouth. It looked as if the flies were performing the Naroo Dance. She was too weak to lift her hand and wave the flies away. The three of them lay there as if dead. The mediapersons, the police, the officers of the Forest Department, their neighbours, the government—no one cared to notice their distress. No god, no caste, no religion stood by them. They lay there like refuse, blinking their dying eyes.

That same day, the villagers of Biripali heard that the

decomposed body of a beast had been discovered in the depths of the forest. The rotten flesh, broken bones and dried-up blood were the only remains that were found. Its claws, teeth and skin were missing. They had miraculously vanished from the spot. It was a tiger all right, the villagers could be seen whispering to one another.

The Aesthetics of a Supercyclone

RUBEN HAD BECOME free of the shackles of time. For the first time, he had discovered himself as someone who enjoyed complete freedom. Whichever way he looked, he saw only himself. Had he been an ordinary individual, Ruben might have suffocated under the pressure of this limitless freedom and might have been forced to kill himself. But he had been transformed into an exceptional human being. He could drink seawater and breathe stench. He did not feel hunger. He could not tell the tastes apart—maybe the taste glands on his tongue no longer functioned. Ruben wasn't sure if his stomach was in its proper place. He felt he had become a detached, shapeless, supine being.

Ruben felt that he was living within the circle of eternal time. He could see himself and his own time from a distance. He felt shame when he thought of his life before the cyclone struck. He had forsaken that life and now lived a new, more exacting, more organized and detached one. He had never imagined that one could play hide-and-seek with one's own life in this manner.

Earlier, he had trained himself to take the dreary and the uncomfortable in his stride. He had reconciled himself to his own sense of inferiority, his poverty and his ignorance. But now he had metamorphosed into a complete man. He now stood alongside God, and felt obliged to him.

God had given him the gift of intellect in lieu of agony, an agony born out of despair and distress. God had breathed new life into him and rejuvenated his aesthetic sense. God had resurrected him, he had made him a guinea pig for his experiments in the laboratory of life. God could dissect Ruben and conduct whichever experiments he desired to. Ruben, for his own part, was amazed at the great change that had come over him all of a sudden. He was amazed by the abundance of energy that seemed to have been infused into him. Ruben experienced a sense of humiliation when he compared the life he enjoyed now to the one he lived earlier. It had never occurred to Ruben that such energy and such great strength had remained locked inside him.

Ruben remembered the storm clearly. It was a black gust of wind, spiralling violently out of a monster's mouth, the way they sometimes show on television. Through the window he had seen an enormous tidal wave rushing at his house. At first he had thought the tide would change its course and move off in some other direction. After all, neither he nor his mother or his sister, Ruby, had done anything wrong. Still, the storm came. The tide wrenched his house off its base and made it spin. The walls and windows of his house, his mother, Ruby, the flowers in the vase, the happiness captured in photo-albums, the love letters from Chumki kept in his bookshelf—everything flew off here and there. Ruben had closed his eyes and kept them tightly shut for a long time but he could feel the storm entering his body from one end and exiting it from the other. Perhaps he had felt himself spinning round and round as he got caught up in that storm—he could not remember that now. A numbness had suddenly gripped him and made him motionless and inert. The storm had passed through all his organs—his bones, his lungs, his liver, his stomach, his intestines—and washed them clean.

Ruben now stood erect; he looked clean and white and transparent. He was free of all blemishes, all flaws. He felt no sensation. He felt no attachment to anybody or anything. He had the power to devour every law, every norm, every rule. He could gulp down all the venom of this world, all the sleeping pills that had ever been produced. He could race ten thousand miles in a single second, overcoming all obstacles.

He had become a unique human being. He could ward off the clouds, the lightning or the sea with a simple wave of his hand. He could effortlessly toss away greed, attachment, libido. He had the confidence to challenge even God. He would toss a coin in the air and ask God: 'Heads or tails? Come on, decide quickly.'

~

When Ruben had opened his eyes, he had been taken aback. There was no sign of his house. Ruby's dead body lay near him. Ruben wondered what a man with his powers should do under these circumstances. Ruby was dead. She would never call out to him again. Of her voice, her footsteps, her childish demands, her pranks and pique, her obstinacy, her dreams, her emotions, worries and anxieties, excitement and tears, nothing remained. Only her lifeless body lay there. Still, the body was there—what should one do with it? Ruben again glanced at his sister lying in a pool of seawater, smeared with dirt and mud. The naked body was partly covered by straw, slime and foam. Ruby held something in a closed fist. The posture in which Ruby's body lay might remind one of the Saraswati in M.F. Husain's painting. What did God have in mind when he deposited Ruby's corpse right next to Ruben? Perhaps he wanted to make woe his permanent companion, Ruben reasoned. But Ruben felt like a man who had been reborn, such a man could only feel grateful to God. No distress could touch him now. Sorrow, anger and despondency had all become redundant for Ruben.

Ruby had been studying hard for her matriculation examinations, but all that was now of a different world. Her maths notebook, her English teacher, her sports instructor, her school building, the desk on which Ruby had written her name with chalk, the school peon who always used to tease her and the headmistress who used to reproach her, the small-time shopkeeper who used to gift Ruby chocolates, bottles of nail polish and greeting cards—no one had survived the storm. What would Ruby's life have been like had she remained alive?

The storm had spared not a single thing which could have borne testimony that a lively and playful girl called Ruby once existed. All her certificates—all those scraps of paper which carried the names of her parents and her date of birth had been swallowed up by the wind. The woman who washed Ruby's clothes, too, had disappeared into the storm. The cyclone had swept away the three-year-old boy who used to live in the neighbourhood and who used to come and play with Ruby every day—that boy who used to lovingly call her Ruby 'Nani'. Ruben's mother, too, had not been spared. She, who used to spend hours combing Ruby's hair and coaxing and cajoling her into eating. She had compelled Ruby to wear a nose ring. What would Ruby have done without her mother? Death had transformed her into an inert mass which somehow resembled M. F. Husain's Saraswati. Someone might remember her for that, at least.

Ruben took his eyes off his sister's body and looked around. He saw a group of people walking towards him; they held aloft a banner which bore the name of their organization.

Ruben thought, A bunch of aimless, idle men has finally found a job—counting dead bodies. They had found sanctuary behind a screen of philanthropy and selflessness. Ruben had earlier been one of them but the cyclone had transformed him into a unique human being. He used to live a life of deceit before the storm. He would deceive himself and shirk responsibilities just the way they did. Ruben had believed that the world was a gigantic marketplace where man himself was a commodity. He had therefore taken steps to make himself an attractive and marketable product. He had moulded himself accordingly. But the storm had made him realize that he was more than a product meant for sale. There was something special about him, something uncommon and exotic. He was different, unique. He could not be one among many—like termites in a colony, racing pointlessly without identity or aim. Ruben decided he would not join the race that went on in this termite-colony of a world.

Therefore, Ruben ran away, leaving his sister's body there. He thought he would look for Chumki. In the next couple of days Ruben peered at about ten thousand bodies, but none of them was Chumki's. Ruben felt neither despair nor depression even after spending two days among the dead. A helicopter hovered overhead and dropped food packets. A packet fell near Ruben. He picked it up, opened and ate a little of its contents; he then handed the packet to a man standing near him. He drank the brackish water, breathed the stinking air, and resumed the game of 'Find Chumki'.

His eyes fell on a group of men dragging a trolley-cart

along the road. It was full of lifeless bodies. One of the corpses looked like his own mother, he thought, but he felt no interest in checking. His father had died a few years earlier. Ruben still remembered the funeral rites. There was a group of five or seven people in the family who had kept lamenting his death. Elderly relatives had never stopped their advice: 'Sleep facing east. Eat only boiled green gram, once a day. Remember to keep the clay lamp burning all the time. Wash the feet of a Brahmin every day and drink that water. Arrange for your father's favourite food to be given to the poor.'

'Father used to smoke ganja and drink every day, what about that?' Ruben had asked.

The question had so infuriated Ruben's maternal uncle that he had left. It had taken three days, the tireless persuasion of two other relatives, and a set of new clothes that cost about one thousand rupees to mollify the uncle and bring him back. Ruben wondered where that uncle was now. Had he been here, Ruben thought, he would have seen how his sister's body was cremated in the modern and scientific way: by first being doused in kerosene and then covered with burning tyres.

Ruben began to run. He ran in a direction that would lead him away from where most of the people were heading. He did not look at anyone, nor did any one bother to notice him. All of them seemed preoccupied and restless. Unlike everyone around him, Ruben was calm and unperturbed. Ruined houses, fallen trees, devastated fields, twisted light posts and remnants of bridges which had been washed away flashed past as he ran on. Dead calves, dead children, dead pigs; live dogs, vultures and hawks—he left all of them behind without stopping.

Ruben kept running—three days, four, seven, eight, ten days—and then stopped. He had reached a bend in the road in a town that looked safe and cosy.

He remembered Chumki. Was she alive? Or had she too died in the cyclone? Some pimp may have forced her into a brothel for all he knew. No sooner did the thought occur to him than Ruben started walking towards the red-light area of the town. A few men approached, thinking him a potential customer.

'Poor men.' Ruben felt a surge of pity for them.

'What do you want, sir?' one of them asked.

'I was in love with a girl. Her name is Chumki. I am looking for her,' Ruben replied.

The pimps left without saying anything more. Ruben wandered in the vicinity for ten more days. One day he saw Chumki at a window; she was combing her hair. She could not see Ruben. All at once, Ruben lost all interest in Chumki. He felt no excitement on seeing her. Why had he spent so many days searching for her? Ruben wondered. Why had he wanted to meet her? What need was there? Why should he disturb her? Let her be, he thought. It is enough to know that she survived.

Ruben came back and started working in a small tea-shop. The owner assigned him sundry jobs. Sometimes, Ruben was asked to serve tea to customers. Sometimes he smiled at them and at other times, he did not. 'What's the problem?' someone would then ask, and Ruben would reply promptly: 'Chumki is the problem.'

People did not understand what he meant. Sometimes, a customer would tease Ruben. 'Has "Chumki" happened to you today? No?' Perhaps it was the recurrent mention of the name Chumki—within a couple of months, the owner changed the name of his shop to 'Chumki Tea Shop'.

Customers thronged. The owner was pleased with Ruben. He was much older than Ruben, but shorter. He had to crane his neck to meet Ruben's eyes when talking to him. One day, he craned his neck, looked Ruben in the eye and said, 'Here, take five thousand rupees. Get me the stuff mentioned on the list.' He also told Ruben, 'Visit a saloon on your way back. Get a decent haircut and a shave, and get your nails clipped, too.' Without a word, Ruben took the money and left. He walked straight to the house where he had seen Chumki at the window. Chumki was shocked. She laughed; then, she cried. She took Ruben inside and sat him on the bed but she did not utter a word about the cyclone. She gazed at Ruben's face. Ruben had lost weight and looked taller. He had not shaved for many days and his nails, too, had grown long. Ruben observed Chumki. As far as he could remember, Chumki did not use lipstick. But that day her lips were painted crimson. She wore a lot of jewellery. She was wearing gaudy and dazzling clothes—a ghagra and a chunri. Her hair, too, was quite striking. It had been trimmed in such a way that it frilled over the upper portion of her forehead. The hair at the back of her head was done up in two long braids. She looked like a character out of an opera party. But Ruben liked her made-up, glamorous look; he enjoyed the perfume flooding the room.

'Do you want something to eat?' Chumki asked, then added, 'there is nothing in the house, let's eat out.' Chumki changed into a light-grey sari—she had no inhibitions about changing in Ruben's presence. The cyclone had blown away shame and embarrassment. It had left no choice for the survivors. Before the cyclone, Chumki would have asked, 'What colour should I wear?' and Ruben would have suggested, 'Wear a coffee-coloured sari, it is cloudy today.' Those tender emotions seemed to have been blown away by the storm. Everything had become banal and crude.

They munched on some snacks in a coffee-shop. Chumki paid the bill and asked, 'Where shall we go from here? The beach?'

Ruben said nothing.

They hired a taxi and went to the beach. They chose a comparatively lonely place and lay down on the sand. Ruben rested his head on Chumki's belly and slept.

The sky was a blend of dark and light blue. A few

patches of white, black and grey clouds sailed lazily across. One or two birds cruised amidst the clouds. The waves undulated and danced in front of their eyes. The heads of the swimmers looked like black spots. A few light boats bobbed up and down. Chumki's eyes were open but she saw nothing. Ruben woke up after an hour or so and called out to Chumki. But she had fallen asleep. Ruben sat up and gazed at the sleeping Chumki. Her parents and two brothers had gone missing after the cyclone. Chumki had taken everything in her stride. She did not talk about herself nor did she ask Ruben any questions. She was not even trying to hide facts or feign ignorance.

Chumki's belly rose rhythmically up and down as she breathed. Ruben played with it a little—he sprinkled some sand, two or three sand-worms scrambled. Chumki woke with a start and flicked them off. She adjusted her sari.

'Ruben, what is inside the human body?' she asked.

'Two hundred and six pieces of bone, arteries and veins, the nervous system and many such things.'

'What else?'

'Nothing else.'

'Where is the soul? Where, in the human body, is the inner being, the conscience, the seat of emotions?'

'They cannot be slotted like that,' Ruben snapped. 'Do you think they are kept in separate canisters like oil, sugar, tea and spices on the kitchen shelf? And to think of the soul is absurd, the only thing that matters is our body. The body is everything. No matter which part gets hurt—the bone or the head or the belly or our sentiments—it is the body that feels the pain. One may have different names for the kinds of pain we feel, but the body feels them all. We are the body! We laugh and our body laughs. If we cry, so does the body.'

The two of them sat silently for a long time and watched the two small children who ran towards the water to touch the waves; sometimes the waves rushed at them and sometimes they rushed at the waves. Their parents sat on the beach. They warned the children from time to time to not get too close to the water. They spoke a language Ruben and Chumki did not know. Sometimes they looked at the sea with big, round eyes and waved their hands with the speed of a flying arrow. Ruben and Chumki guessed that they had come from a place that was far away from the cyclone-affected areas. Now both rose to their feet, walked to the road and hailed a taxi. 'Where to?' Chumki asked Ruben. Ruben gave the driver the address of a shop. It took the taxi ten minutes to reach. 'Wait here, I'll be back in two minutes,' Ruben told Chumki. He came back after some time and got back inside the taxi. He was holding a small packet. 'Chumki Tea Shop,' Ruben told the driver. Chumki cast a curious look at the packet. Ruben asked her to open it. Chumki gave a start when she saw the small pistol inside the packet. Ruben had bought it with the five thousand rupees the tea-shop-owner had given him.

'What will you do with it?' Chumki asked in a puzzled voice.

'It gives one the courage to challenge God,' Ruben replied mysteriously.

Chumki looked confused but kept quiet. The taxi pulled up in front of Chumki Tea Shop. The two of them got down. Ruben paid the driver and he drove away. Ruben looked at his master, the shop-owner. He looked angry; after all, Ruben had been away the whole day and had now returned without a single article mentioned on the list. But he did not say anything because there was a girl with Ruben. Some of the customers who sat lazily sipping tea, looked at Ruben and Chumki with curiosity in their eyes.

'This is Chumki,' Ruben said. 'She will work here.'

The shop-owner gave him a startled look. Chumki stood silently. The shop-owner glanced at her. Holding two cups of tea he walked close to Ruben and spoke in his ear. He asked Ruben about the five thousand rupees he had given him in the morning. Ruben opened the packet and showed him the pistol. 'I bought this with the money,' he said nonchalantly.

The cups fell from the shop-owner's hands. His head began to spin. He slowly walked behind the counter and slumped in his chair. He tried his best to look away from Ruben. He forgot that Ruben had come to his shop with an unknown girl. The hot tea had fallen on his feet but he felt no pain. He forgot the customers sitting in the shop. He could no longer be sure if it was day or night.

Ruben poured out two cups of tea for himself and Chumki. When he offered tea to the shop-owner, he shook his head and gestured with his hand for some water instead. 'I will now take Chumki back to her house,' Ruben said. 'She will start working here from tomorrow—day shift only.' The shop-owner stared blankly at Ruben and nodded.

Long after Ruben and the girl had left, the shopkeeper was still trying to compose himself and think clearly. But his limbs trembled, his heart beat erratically, and his head reeled. 'Maybe I should close the shop early tonight and go home. No, no, I will close down the shop permanently.' But he was in no shape to take any decision. Only recently had business started to pick up and the number of customers increased in the evening hours. The poor shop-owner was thoroughly shaken by the unexpected turn of events. Finally, he seemed to make up his mind. 'I shall close down the shop tomorrow,' he muttered. Then, addressing some customers at the shop, he said aloud, 'Sir, Chumki Tea Shop will remain closed from tomorrow.'

'No, I will close it tonight itself,' he said to himself after some time. He announced loudly: 'You must forgive me, good sirs, but you will not get any more tea tonight.' Within half an hour, he had put away everything in the room and slammed the bolt shut. He searched for the bunch of keys to lock the door. He lifted the cushion of his seat. The bunch was under the cushion and beside it lay the pistol. At the sight of the pistol the fellow jumped back in fear. He turned abruptly and found Ruben standing close to him. He felt life draining out of his body. Ruben stared at the shop-owner in silence. Instead of locking the door, he handed the keys over to Ruben. 'I am leaving,' he said to Ruben and quickly left. Ruben entered the room, closed and bolted the door from the inside. Around midnight, a single gunshot rang out from within Ruben's room. When Ruben opened the door early the following morning, he found two policemen and four stupid-looking fellows wearing monkey-caps standing outside. They stared at Ruben and asked, 'Murder? Or suicide?'

Ruben called them inside and explained what exactly had happened. He had removed a nice glass-framed photograph of the shop-owner from the wall. He had then put it on the toilet pan and shot at it from a close range, aiming at the man's heart. Thereafter, Ruben said, he had gone to sleep. The men, who considered themselves experts, began examining the room. They inquired about the pistol. Ruben said that he had the pistol with him but would not give it to them. Chumki arrived at that moment. She radiated a soothing warmth, like the soft sunlight of a winter morning. Her presence comforted everybody except Ruben. The hostile-looking policemen softened. They pulled a couple of chairs out and sat down. 'Who is the girl?' one of them asked. Ruben answered that she was his friend and that she lived in the slums in the red-light area of the town. He also told them that the girl worked in the tea-shop. Ruben then asked the policeman to stand up.

The policemen stared at Ruben uncomprehendingly.

'Come on, get off the chairs, you scoundrels,' Ruben shouted as he pointed the pistol at them. Neither the policemen, nor the other four; not even Chumki could understand what was happening.

Ruben spoke, his tone casual and light. 'There are only two chairs here. I will sit in one and God will sit in the other. No one except God has the right to sit beside me.' He paused, then began, 'I shall now play God's favourite game.' He sat down in one of the chairs; he asked Chumki to stand behind him. He ordered the policemen to strip and pointed the gun at them. Frightened, the policemen began to take their clothes off. Ruben fired a shot in the air. It scared the policemen out of their wits and they scrambled to undress.

Ruben ordered the men to parade in the room. 'Savdhan! Vishram! March on, you scoundrels!' he barked. The naked policemen marched out of the room and ran away. Ruben closed the door and flopped down on the bed. He called Chumki to his side. 'Do you know, they have organized a ceremony today for all those who died in the cyclone. There will be a yagna.'

'Yes, thousands of people have started arriving at the ground to watch it,' Chumki said. A shiver ran through Ruben's body. Within a second he jumped down from the bed, took the pistol out, locked the door and began running towards the ground. Chumki ran behind him. He pushed and prodded the jostling crowd and walked up to the altar where the holy fire was burning. He fired ten rounds at it and then rushed to the place where fifty-odd priests in saffron robes, their heads shaven, stood in front of the microphone, chanting hymns. Ruben fired ten more shots and ordered the priests to take their clothes off.

'Savdhan! Vishram! Savdhan! Vishram! Run! Run!' he shouted at the top of his voice. 'Run—run, you parasites!' The shaven-headed priests started to run around the ground and Ruben ran after them, pistol in hand. He made them run two rounds. The confused crowd scattered; people were shocked out of their wits at this unexpected turn of events. Ruben also ran after them and into the middle of the crowd. He was heard saying, 'Friends, I am a free man. God has sent me to punish you. Do you know God has sent man to earth to start life from the lowest point of agony and despair? He intends to make man pass through ordeals and test his potential. God wants to see if man is capable of freeing himself from the bondage of worldly attachments. God is conducting experiments on man. Why do you people add to his troubles through your deceit? God has not sanctioned any specified religion to any specific sect; he has not given any moral lessons nor has he asked man to abide by them. Why do you people act as middlemen between God and man? Why do you exploit innocent people in the name of God and religion? Why don't you leave them alone and let them shoulder the responsibility of building their own lives? Why do you force them into self-deception?'

A couple of bullets hit Ruben and he fell. The police sent his dead body for post-mortem and seized his weapon. They noticed that it was a toy pistol.

Two days after Ruben's death, the tea-shop re-opened. Under the signboard that announced the name, 'Chumki Tea Shop', each letter written in a different colour, sat Chumki. The shop was crowded with customers. Two waiters were busy serving tea. The pleasant sound of cups and saucers clinking filled the air. Chumki's face was lit up with a happy smile. She looked like the beatific Mohini who emerged during the mythical churning of the ocean. Like Mohini, who held the pot of nectar as well as that of venom in her hands, Chumki radiated a pristine charm.

The Testimony of God

PREMASHILA'S SEVEN-YEAR-OLD son died on the train. Mother and son were travelling to their village from Hyderabad along with some daily-wage labourers whom she worked with in the city. The boy had been suffering from fever for the last three days. Someone had given her a tablet to bring down the temperature, and she had somehow made her son swallow it, but Premashila could not be sure if the temperature was actually coming down or rising. Over the two-day journey, she had given her son only a few bananas and some tea.

Sometime in the night, Premashila touched her son. He felt unusually cold and stiff. Her heart lurched violently. She looked around and found everyone asleep. She lay down by his side and shed silent tears. A feeling of emptiness numbed her senses; she couldn't think or see anything clearly. Her hand strayed to the waist-fold of her sari where she had kept two thousand rupees in a tightly knotted bundle; she had earned this amount in the six months she had spent working in Hyderabad. It was still six or seven hours before the train would reach the railway station near her village and she lay beside her dead son, careful not to make any sound.

In the morning someone asked, 'Has the fever come down?'

Premashila shook her head but didn't say anything. The man reached out to feel the boy's forehead but she stopped him. 'Let him sleep,' she said. A few others came up to her before the train reached and wanted to know if the boy's fever had come down. Premashila shook her head each time and didn't utter a word.

She was afraid. They would all loot her hard-earned money if they learnt that her son had died. The vultures would suck the last paisa out of her; first, the broker who had employed her; the Railways police would pounce upon her next; then the station master, the guard, the rickshawala, the doctor and, finally, the town police would take turns to harass her. She would not have even ten or twenty rupees left at the end of the day to cremate the body.

She hoisted her son on to her shoulder with much difficulty, careful not to let anyone know that he had died. Despite the precautions she took, a man by her side, his eyes wide with suspicion, looked at her once and then at her son. But he did not say anything.

Instead of trying to harden her heart, Premashila made it as light and soft as cotton-wool. Her eyes held a vacant look, there were no tears in them. She moved nervously, slowly, towards the exit gate of the platform, fearing that any moment the vultures would swoop down and snatch away her son's body. There was no one around. She exited through the gate but before she could take even a step forward, the vultures appeared out of nowhere and descended upon her. Premashila felt faint. The world before her dry, tearless eyes went blank. She shut her eyes.

When she came to—she didn't know after how long—Premashila found herself in a police station. Her son was no longer on her shoulder and when she reached for the waist-fold of her sari she found nothing there. Her bundle had disappeared, too.

She had had this same experience two years earlier when her husband had died on the platform of Vishakhapatnam Railway Station. Her husband's body couldn't reach home even after she had spent all her money. Premashila didn't try to remember where and how he eventually vanished.

Premashila didn't know why she was kept in the lockup. There, they took her thumb impression on several pieces of paper. Only much later did she find that a criminal case had been filed against her, that she had been accused of murdering her son. She was made to stand in the dock and explain why she had committed such a terrible crime. There were a number of nightmarish journeys from the courtroom to jail and from jail back to the courtroom during the six months or so which followed her arrest. Later, she heard, though not very distinctly, that the verdict on her case would be pronounced the following day. Her dazed mind couldn't fathom what she was being accused of. Everything seemed blurred. The only images which made an impression through the numbing haze which surrounded Premashila was that of a flock of hungry vultures, a dense crowd swirling about her, and an immense void.

Soon, though, events took an unexpected turn.

~

One morning, a gentleman wearing a track suit and sneakers opened the front gate of the sessions judge's house and stepped inside. His hands were hidden within gloves and a wide-brimmed white hat covered his head. The judge's servant emerged and looked askance at the man.

'I have come to meet the judge,' the gentleman said. 'I want to discuss a case with him.'

The servant asked the man his name.

'I am God. I have come from heaven.'

He is trying to bully me, the servant thought, but did not say anything. He cast a quick glance at the wide-brimmed hat and the gloves and went into the house. He came out again after a few minutes, accompanied by an old man.

'Yes, what can I do for you?' the judge asked.

The man who had introduced himself as God said without preamble, 'I understand that you are going to sentence the woman to seven years. I am here to discuss certain things related to the case.'

The judge was shocked. How does this man know this? he wondered. Did the steno pass the information on to him? Maybe he is a lawyer.

'May I know who you are?' he asked aloud.

'I am God. I have come from heaven. I know all about Premashila's case.'

Inwardly, the judge was a little irritated. An advocate wouldn't answer in such a silly fashion, he thought to himself. This must be a man out to make mischief. The judge had no intention of continuing the discussion. 'Come to court at exactly eleven in the morning tomorrow and say whatever you want to say.' He said this in a dismissive tone and went back inside his house.

At eleven a.m. the following day the courtroom was packed to overflowing. Premashila stood in the wooden dock on one side of the room, her gaze fixed on nothing. Her dry eyes caught blurred, occasional glimpses of black coats, black heads and black faces but her mind couldn't register a thing. Facing her, and standing in the dock on the other side of the court room, stood the gentleman in the track suit and the wide-brimmed white hat. Since no one looked at him, he probably had not drawn anyone's notice.

The judge walked in and everyone stood up. Everyone sat down once he took his seat. As soon as the judge's eyes fell on the man in the track suit he asked the advocates, 'Do you recognize this man? Is he your witness, complainant or client?' The people in the courtroom looked at one another. Then they looked at the gentleman, and their curious eyes appraised his outfit. But no one said anything.

'Who is your advocate?' the judge asked the man in the dock.

'I haven't one.'

'Who put you in the dock?'

'No one. I came here on my own.'

'Will you introduce yourself?'

'I am God. I have come from heaven.'

A loud uproar filled the room. The judge struck his gavel and ordered everyone to be silent.

'You are wasting the court's time with such rubbish.'

'No, what I say is true.'

'Why should we believe that you are God?'

'The existence of God need not be proved. It is a question of faith. Besides, you and everybody else in this court can see me standing here.'

'But the court needs evidence. You have to substantiate your claim.'

'What kind of proof do you want?'

'Well…' The judge thought for a moment. 'Tell us the names of your parents, your caste, the name of your town or village. The court would like to see your voter card, ration card or driving licence. The court also will need to know your address, everything about your job if you work in some office or institution, or about your business if you are a businessman—things like that.'

'My address? I live in heaven. It cannot be proved, since that is also a question of faith. I don't possess any of those documents you just mentioned.'

'Does God wear a track suit, sneakers, gloves and hat?' the judge asked sarcastically and laughed. Everyone except Premashila joined him in laughter.

'I wear whatever I want. God never wears a uniform.' The man who called himself God replied, completely unfazed by the laughter.

By now the judge was visibly annoyed.

'Please leave now,' he demanded and, in a louder voice, repeated, 'You are wasting the court's time.'

'How can I leave? I haven't said anything about Premashila yet. In fact, that is the reason why I have come here,' the man in the track suit said with mild stubbornness.

This man is not normal, the judge thought. For a brief moment he considered handing the man over to the police but decided on second thought to give him a hearing. 'Okay, I can give you two minutes. You have to say what you want to say within that time. But before that you have to swear in the name of God that you will tell the truth and nothing but the truth.'

'How very strange!' the gentleman exclaimed. 'How can I swear in my own name? Only human beings do so. But you can trust me; rest assured that I will tell only the truth.'

'No.' The judge shook his head. 'You have to abide by the rules of the court. You have to swear and, further, you have to furnish proof of your identity,' he declared with an air of finality.

'You are asking me for my proof of identity yet again. What proof should I give you?'

'Give us a miracle, okay? Keep this paperweight hanging in the air,' said the judge, picking one up from his table. 'Everyone will witness that.'

Then, it happened—

As everyone looked on in breathless silence, the paperweight slipped out of the judge's hand and hung in the air. Then it started to spin around the courtroom at great speed. The people were scared out of their wits. The advocates lowered their heads, fearing that the hurtling paperweight might slam into them. There were seven more such paperweights on the judge's table and all of them began to spin in the air. 'Your Honour, you accept the revolving of these seven tiny paperweights as proof of my existence. What do you have to say about the nine enormous paperweights hanging in space for ages?' the man who called himself God asked amusedly.

The judge broke into a sweat and his throat parched. He drank a glass of water and tried to calm his nerves. But his rational mind could not completely dismiss lingering doubts. He might be a magician for all you know, he told himself.

He waited for a while and asked, 'Can you make it rain? Now?'

God smiled. He did not say anything but a storm sprang up. The wind tore about the room in violent gusts and rain poured in torrents. People tried to grab at the sheets of paper that flew around the courtroom to prevent them from getting drenched. Some tried to run but could not. All the doors were closed and nobody could open them. The floor of the courtroom splashed with water six inches deep. Everyone except God and Premashila were drenched. Their clothes, their shoes, socks and wristwatches—everything was soaked by the rain. Files and papers floated about in the water even as the rain kept pouring with force. Everyone was frightened.

'Shall I stop the rain?' God asked the judge.

'Please,' the judge begged. 'Please.'

The rain ceased as abruptly as it had begun. Everyone in the court stood paralyzed by a nameless fear. Premashila alone was in the dock, unmoved, unaffected by everything that was happening around her.

'Do you need any more proof?' God asked the judge.

The judge swallowed to ease his dry throat. 'No,' he said hoarsely.

'Now, should I say something about the accused?' God asked. The judge couldn't speak. He merely waved his hand about twice, indicating an adjournment. He rose slowly from his chair and was about to leave when something strange happened.

He saw that everyone had knelt on the water-logged floor of the courtroom and was praying. 'God, please forgive us. We know what a heinous crime we have committed. We are ready to return Premashila's money with interest. Please forgive us.'

A blinding flash of lightning lit up the room and an earsplitting thunderclap filled the air. The people gathered felt as if the lightning and thunder spanned the insides of their heads. They screwed their eyes shut and it was only after two minutes or so that they could open them.

They saw that the dock where God had stood was now empty. Some people lay near the dock, unconscious. Premashila found that all the hawks and vultures who had circled her lay scattered all around.

The honourable judge declared that the judgement would be pronounced the following day and warned the culprits that all of the money due to Premashila should be deposited with him before the session began.

An envelope stuffed with Premashila's money reached the judge's house before he left for court the following day.

The judge delivered his verdict exactly at eleven a.m. 'Premashila is guilty of murder. She is to be hanged until dead,' he declared solemnly and, without breaking the nib as he signed the papers, he re-capped his fountain pen and put it back in his pocket. After the verdict the judge went on indefinite leave.

Premashila stood in the dock and heard the judge read out the verdict. Her face registered no expression. She appeared not to have understood even a word of what she had heard.

The Dreamer's Tale

HE HAD JUST woken up from a nap filled with dreams, which was why his heart was heavy with sorrow.

He had left his village, and his home in it, and headed for another. He walked past the outskirts of his village and along the highway, looking at farms, barns, the lush vegetation and the green pastures which stretched out on both sides of the road. A horse stormed past him. The dreamer noticed that a young and handsome man rode it; perhaps he was a prince. The horse had glossy, sparkling white skin. It galloped on at great speed, as if it was flying. It raced past cornfields, woodlands, the highway and the people on it, and disappeared beyond the horizon.

The dreamer drifted into another spell.

If only he had such a beautiful horse. If only he had been so handsome. His horse would have been white. No, black. No, red of course. White is easily dirtied. Black was no better, it suits a bear or a ghost. Red was best. Yes.

He mounted the horse dressed in a bright red outfit;

onlookers were blinded by the dazzle as his horse trotted along. They rubbed their eyes, looked admiringly at him, and wondered, 'Who is this prince?'

The horse trotted gently in the beginning and gradually picked up speed. It eventually gathered so much momentum that it soared off the ground. People craned their necks and stared at him. He flew past towns, trees, mountains, oceans and clouds in the blink of an eye. He could not imagine any further because he had no idea what lay beyond the clouds. And he was a little skeptical about taking a trip to the moon or the stars. So he took a turn instead and got the horse to land on earth. He alighted and looked around for water. He was breathing hard, his throat was burning with thirst. Completely drained, he rested by the roadside and then began looking for water again. He might or might not have found water, but his dream had not yet ended.

The scene changed—

There was no sign of the red horse, nor was he himself in the gorgeous red outfit. He saw that he was wearing a shabby brown dress. There were two pairs of pockets in it—one pair in the shirt and the other in the trousers. He decided he would get all of eight pockets stitched in the red outfit after he got it back. He would stow away his valuables in them. He might receive a number of expensive gifts or acquire a lot of money; he might even—if fortune favoured him—lay his hand on priceless gems. He might come across many unseen, strange and wonderful objects. The pockets would come in handy then.

He continued to dream—

His desire to own the red horse grew stronger and stronger. If only I could own that majestic horse! he thought wistfully. He was now determined to own a horse just like that. He stopped a passerby to ask him about the animal, but turned to wood in fear at the sight of the unusually large moustache the man sported. It was thick and big and the twisted ends on both sides reached up all the way to the ears. The dreamer was confused and, instead of asking the man how much a red horse might cost, asked, 'How much does this moustache cost?' The man with the strange moustache did not reply; he only cast a glance at the dreamer and walked away. Perhaps he thought the dreamer was mad.

After a while, the dreamer came across another man. He called out to him. When the man came close the dreamer noticed that he had a cobra coiled around his neck; the snake raised its hood and glared at the dreamer. The sight stunned the dreamer and the question he had intended to ask the passerby was forgotten. He took two quick steps back and stood wide-eyed, watching the man and the cobra around his neck. The man with the cobra grinned and went away.

The dreamer heaved a sigh of relief. He, too, walked on. He decided he would not ask anyone about the horse; he would just have to look for it himself. After a few minutes, he came across a stable. A few horses were grazing in the field nearby. 'This must be my destination,' the dreamer said to himself. He moved a little closer. A place that looked like a hermitage caught his eye; he saw people milling about in it. He was not sure if it would be wise to ask anyone anything. Therefore, he stood at a distance and silently observed the scene. Everyone wore a grim expression, everyone was busy. No one bothered to smile at him.

The dreamer stood for quite some time. Then he summoned courage and waved at a man and asked him to come closer. The man came up to the dreamer, put a mark on his forehead with some holy powder, and looked questioningly at him. The dreamer explained that he had come to buy a horse. The man asked the dreamer to follow him and entered the hermitage. There, a large crowd had gathered. The dreamer looked around in wonder. A number of men in red and saffron cloaks, their heads shaven, moved about in the spacious courtyard. He could not be sure if there were women among these monks—they all looked so alike! The monk who walked with the dreamer led him to their 'guru'. They walked down narrow passages, across several courtyards and climbed several steps to finally arrive at the Baba's seat.

The dreamer was quite taken with the Baba's looks— he was so tall, so powerfully built, so graceful! And he wore his hair so long! The dreamer could not take his eyes off the holy man. The dreamer was asked to genuflect before the Baba so he lay prostrate and, before anyone could say anything, muttered, 'A horse!' Four shaven-headed men in saffron gowns whispered into the long-haired Baba's ear; the Baba, too, answered in a whisper; then he closed his eyes and stood silently for some time. One of the saffron-robed men up came to the dreamer and whispered something in his ear. The dreamer stared at him in surprise. 'Fifty thousand rupees!' he uttered disbelievingly.

The Baba opened his eyes, raised his hands above his head and began chanting some mantras. Then he closed his hand into a fist and asked the dreamer to stretch out his hands. The Baba opened his fist and an egg fell into the open palms of the surprised dreamer. The dreamer was very impressed. He wondered, awestruck, How did the holy man produce an egg out of nowhere? The Baba closed his eyes once more and muttered some slokas in Sanskrit. He then signalled to some of his disciples. Four men came up to the dreamer, caught hold of him, dragged him into another room and frisked him. One strange object after another came out of the dreamer's pockets—tiger's whiskers, a shell, a small conch, scales of the vajrakapta reptile, bird feathers, four pebbles from a river bank, a rudraksh bead, a piece of musk, children's toys, crumpled paper boats, balloons, the petals of a withered flower, stones, sand. The saffron-robed men were astonished and amused at the sight; laughing, they put the objects back into the dreamer's pockets. One of them twisted his ears while another pulled at his hair.

One of them brought a white gourd and ordered the dreamer to scoop out its pulp. The dreamer laboured for an hour and removed the pulp from inside the white gourd; the shaven-headed men then asked him to place the egg inside the empty shell of the gourd. The dreamer obeyed. Another monk brought hay and wrapped it tight around the white gourd. 'Hold this carefully,' he warned the dreamer. 'Keep it near the hearth from sunrise to sunset for five days. Place it in such a way so that it can catch heat directly from the hearth. Take care lest a cat or a mouse should roll it away. Take a bath before sunrise, focus your mind on Baba and offer up prayers to him. Smear the holy powder on your body and lash yourself twice with a cane. After sunset on the fifth day, walk slowly to a cornfield, holding the gourd with extreme care. Find a lonely spot, untie the cord and remove the straw wrapping. A baby horse will come out of the gourd. Mind you, the colt will start sprinting about as soon as it is released. You must catch it immediately or it will run away. Remember, it is the colt of a winged-horse, come to earth thanks only to the blessings of Baba. It has not been born from its mother's womb. For ten days, it must be fed only milk. Thereafter, feed it grass, gram and gruel. Its wings will grow after six months. Wait for another six months. You can ride the horse only after it is a year old. Before that its bones will be tender and may break under your weight. Wash its back and its wings with milk, never let flies near it. The winged horse will be milky white in colour.'

'Can't you make it red?' the dreamer interjected.

'Well… Perhaps if it is fed enough gram, and if you have Baba's blessings, its colour will change to red,' the monk said encouragingly.

The dreamer was delighted and got up to leave but, before he could do so, the monks forced him to undergo a series of squats. He had to perform squats no less than ten times and hold his ears as he did so. Then, a monk took a cane and lashed the dreamer a couple of times. 'These are the Baba's blessings,' he said. 'Now you can go. May you prosper!'

The dreamer got up. His body was bruised and sore from the beating but he was happy. He lifted the gourd with its straw wrapping and walked out of the hermitage in a relaxed mood, pleased that he would not have to spend any money to own a horse. He returned to his wreck of a hut on the outskirts of the town, lit a fire in the hearth and warmed the gourd for five days. He bought lots of horse gram and stored it even though he himself had to go without food. Occasionally, he touched the hay covering the gourd to check if it was warm.

On the fifth day the weather became cloudy and it rained intermittently. Water dripped down the eaves to the courtyard. The roof of his house began to leak and a few drops of water fell into the hearth. The dreamer was worried. It was a matter of just one more day. How could he make sure the gourd and the egg inside it remained safe?

All the firewood he had stored had become soaked. Now he was upset. He stood up, joined his hands in reverence and offered his salutations to Baba. Then he went through the ritual of squats. Having completed ten rounds of the exercise he brought out a cane and beat himself with it. 'O noble one! I pray for your blessings,' he said. The rain stopped miraculously after two hours and the sun came out. He put some firewood out to dry in the sun. After some time he put the partly dry firewood in the hearth. He set fire to it and blew air on them with a blowpipe. He set the hay-wrapped gourd very close to the fire to have it warmed comparatively quickly. Suddenly the hay covering caught fire. He sprinkled water on the gourd. He also tried to put the fire out with his hands, badly burning them in the process. But he was happy in spite of all this because the last day was drawing to a close. The sun had started its journey down the western skies.

As twilight was giving way to night, the dreamer walked slowly towards a deserted field carrying the white gourd on his shoulders. The gourd felt slightly heavier that day; perhaps the baby horse had come out of its shell, the dreamer thought happily. At the same time, he felt a little nervous. Who knew what fate had in store for him! If only it hadn't rained on this last day of the hatching! And the straw wrapping had to catch fire today! the dreamer fretted.

It was pitch dark when the dreamer reached his destination. One could scarcely make out the earthen ridge which separated the field from the adjoining one. He had stepped on thorns on his way here; he had also slipped a couple of times. He clutched the gourd to his chest with all his strength and walked with extreme care on the slippery track. Still, one of his feet slipped and and he fell into a pit. The white gourd smashed into four pieces. The dreamer felt sick with fear and started groping for the colt with panic-stricken hands. His eyes fell on an animal running away, its eyes glittering in the darkness. It was the colt rushing off at great speed, he realized. He, too, started running after it. Soon, neither the animal that ran ahead nor the man who was chasing it could be seen in the thick darkness of the night.

Dear readers, the story of the dreamer comes to an end here.

The animal which ran away was actually a jackal which had been hiding in the pit. But we cannot explain this to the dreamer because he is now lost in the depths of darkness.

One Thousand Days in a Refrigerator

'WOULD YOU LIKE a story, Lara?' I ask tenderly. Then, without waiting for an answer, say, 'Okay, today I will tell you one about Eskimos.'

Lara lies inert, like the dead, on a white bed in a cold chamber, looking sightlessly at no one knows what. Sounds must enter her ears but they do not reach her brain. Her mouth remains slightly open, revealing— rather grotesquely—the entire upper row of teeth. It is not easy to tell if she is asleep or awake—she has been lying like this for the last five hundred days, her face and body partially hidden by the tubes which connect the various parts of her body to different machines. There is a tube in each nostril, five tubes are connected to her head, two to her chest, another two to her waist and one to her right hand. A dozen in total—I count time and again. She lies like the dead in the cold chamber, seeing nothing, hearing nothing, feeling nothing.

'You know, the Eskimos are a strange people and have strange customs. They send off the oldest member of the family into permanent exile. This sounds strange, doesn't it? But that is how it is. As a matter of fact, one can get old at any age between forty to sixty years. It is up to the individual to maintain equilibrium between his physical condition and his state of mind. But let me come back to my story. The Eskimos observe a ceremony before the fellow sets off on his final journey. He receives a farewell gift of a woolen coat and cap, a woolen scarf, and a pair of warm trousers. They give him knee-high boots and gloves and, with a great deal of affection, put an old overcoat over him. The old fellow is given a sumptuous meal of meat and whale-fat and soup and hot tea. Choking with emotion, they tell him, "Father, may your journey to the other world be well and safe. We, too, will follow you when the time comes." The old man raises his gnarled, quivering hands and blesses everybody. He stammers some final advice: about keeping a torchlight ready for emergencies, about conserving salt, about the nature and movement of snow dunes, about blizzards and avalanches. He tries to speak about stars and candles on dark nights and advises womenfolk to keep knitting woolen stockings. In the end, when he can speak no more, the old man motions to the people that they should cry no more and totters out, his emaciated arms resting on the necks and shoulders of his sons and kinsmen.

'Then, the journey begins. The old man and a few others drag laboured steps through snow and slush, past ice dunes, past crevasses in the ice and over frozen lakes. The women of the family accompany them for a kilometre or so. Then they stop and keep watching the group of men till they vanish into the endless desert of ice.

'After trekking a long, long way, the men in the group sit the old man close to the mouth of a dark cave. They kneel to pray and to weep. After shedding tears for a while they get up and walk home. No one turns to look at the old man sitting forlorn, terrified. They are expressly forbidden by custom from doing that. This happens very rarely but, having travelled a fair distance, someone in the group, driven by irrepressible curiosity, steals a quick glance. He sees—or rather, imagines—the old man, his neck clamped in the jaws of an enormous white creature—which could be a polar bear or an angel—being dragged into the cave. His teeth chatter in fright and later, surrounded by a throng of curious villagers, the man manages only a few indistinct words: "I saw an angel!" '

~

Lara has been lying like the dead in the cold chamber for five hundred days. Nothing touches her, nothing penetrates the boundaries of her conscious perception.

The nurse's gentle touch, or the doctor's advice.

The distress of the people around her or the demands they make of her.

The slivers of silver moonlight, struggling to sneak through the glass panels of her window.

The teasing splash of rain.

—Her brain registers nothing.

The sun or a butterfly on a grey wall.

A spider or a witch…

Pain, pleasure, ache, anguish…

Taste, touch, smell, speech, sight, sound…

Retching, yawning, phlegm-spewing, coughing, wheezing, hiccupping…

—Everything is beyond her.

She senses nothing…

Not the vital air which enters her through the artificial respiratory system and keeps her alive.

Light breaths or deep sighs.

The food fed to her through the tube.

The thunderclap resounding across the sky.

—Nothing finds entry into Lara's consciousness.

~

The long, endless hours I spend with Lara in the refrigerator sometimes fill me with a sense of transcendent claustrophobia—I am hemmed in by walls yet am beyond them.

I touched her gently. 'Lara, your parents were here today. They asked me why I had submitted an application to the hospital authorities to have all the tubes disconnected. They shook with anger. They cursed and shouted, pleaded with me and wept inconsolably. "We will bear all the expenses, let the tubes remain connected," they said.'

'You are all out of your minds,' I said to them. 'Do you think you are Bill Gates's children? Why are you so obsessed with immortality? Why are you so desperate to be elevated to the status of a fake God? Even Bill Gates cannot ask that his wife be made immortal, paying whatever it costs to make such a thing possible. Immortality is reserved exclusively for the gods. No scientist, no Bill Gates, no government will ever succeed in achieving immortality—it remains reserved only for the gods. And, what does "we will meet all expenses" mean? Is it a statement meant to prove your love for your daughter? Is it a futile wish to help her attain immortality? Is it madness?' I shouted at length. They wept some more, cursed me some more, and finally went away, seemingly heartbroken.

Poor human being. How desperate to approach immortality. How very anxious to buy certificates which prove his love and affection. How ridiculously eager to play the role of God. Yet without power. And inescapably trapped by his own limitations.

Tell me, Lara, why do you think a poor man is prepared to sell his kidney to a wealthy patient? Is he guided by selflessness, the thought that the recipient of his organ will attain a fresh lease on life at the cost of his own? I will tell you what prompts him: poverty. His helplessness which does not let him escape the trap of life. Why merely the kidney? You can take my healthy heart if you can pay a good price for it. Money for my red blood, my coffee-coloured liver. Why stop? For more money, I will sell you my arteries and my veins, and all the other organs of my body. Live long. Get as close to immortality as you can. And in the end, if it is possible to exchange your sick brain with mine with the help of your money, you can do that too and achieve the ultimate: immortality! I will be happy for you and for myself, too. I can live for a few more days on your money: I can buy medicines for my wife, clothes for my son, a BPL card for my family, I can knock on God's door and buy smiles for everyone. We can afford charity, contribute to a kinsman's funeral and, having contributed, feel proud and elevated. What do we demand from life other than basic amenities and a bare minimum comfort? For people like us, this minimum privilege is the economic principle on which the concept of immortality stands poised. And it is this principle of economics which assures a healthy, lavish and eternal life for the rich upper classes. However, it is up to earth and to God in heaven to let the principle endure.

Tell me, Lara, would you honestly want anyone to trade his vital organs to help you defy death?

Your parents want to buy you a fresh lease on life with everything they possess. They have already sold their house, their lands and their jewellery to keep you alive. They will not hesitate to sell away their livelihoods, their very lives should the need arise. That is how they dote upon you. Aren't you their precious child?

This is the height of absurdity. Lara, are you really alive?

They would sell their kidneys and their liver, their blood and their bones when they had nothing left to sell. And how much time would they buy their daughter? A hundred, two hundred, five hundred days in the refrigerator? How can they be so dumb? Is all this merely self-deception?

I wonder how you live in the refrigerator. How you must be missing the students whom you taught with such passion, the rickshaw-puller who would regularly take you to school, your bank account, your cheque-book. There is nothing here to hold your interest, neither the jasmine bloom nor the butterflies which you like so much. There are no clothes, no nail-enamel in your favourite shades, no smile in your eyes; the wetness of your lips is gone, as is the soft naughty hiss which sometimes escapes them.

Every dream and emotion, memory and fancy, which froze the day you entered the refrigerator, has long since melted and sloughed away down the drain. There you lie, your face a mask, a mess of tubes, your mouth perpetually frozen in a lopsided, imbecilic smile which bares all your front teeth. No sound or sight can trigger even a minor epiphany within you.

I salute you, my dear, I salute your composure.

~

The nurse tells me that a meeting of the directors of the medical board has been called today to take a decision on the request I made. I presume the board will give its consent. In that case, you will be out of the refrigerator in a day or two. You will not be in this world anymore. A chill creeps over me. My knees feel weak and my head spins. Should I request the office to return my application?

My thoughts travel back in time, to a thousand days earlier, when you were admitted to this ICU. I was not allowed in for the first five hundred days. We would talk for hours over the telephone, through the glass partition which separated us, trying desperately to build a sense of closeness. Then you slipped into a coma and I was allowed admission. Perhaps the medical authorities did not approve of the way we talked to each other for hours together and refused me admission. Or did they decide that having lived out your days in the igloo it is now time for you to travel to the mouth of the cave?

I think Death affects human beings on both tangible and intangible levels. It is tangible when we see Death in the lifeless body of a loved one; we sense it on the intangible level in our memory and in our aching heart where the dead one exists as a non-being. Strangely, when I see you lying here, I can sense you in both ways. I don't know if you are alive or dead. You are with me yet also within my memory...

~

We have remained strangers even after fifteen years of marriage. There is nothing odd in that. On the contrary, it is quite common and happens with many couples. Two human beings may live together for a long time thinking that they know each other well but suddenly, quite unexpectedly, they discover that they have drifted apart—like we did. Each blames the other and what one believes is right the other rejects as wrong. We have been living mentally apart for so many years. Yet, despite the divide, you cooked me my favourite dishes and worried when I fell ill. You applied antiseptic ointment to the wound at the corner of my toe-nail with great care. You never failed to remind me to take pills for hypertension and got terribly upset if I was late. You sent me texts: jokes and romantic messages. Yet, strangely enough, we preferred to remain confined to our respective professional environments when in office. Neither of us ever made any effort to step across the lines and boundaries set down by our own self-esteem and make contact, even though we understood that our egos had wrought havoc with our conjugal life.

Then your epileptic stroke. The shameful irony is that it finally relieved me of the perpetual torment of watching your untrammelled interaction with your superiors. The interaction which prompted them to treat a professional relationship as a means of recreation. It would also, I thought with relief, put a full stop to the dirty comments my colleagues used to make about you and your superiors. One of my colleagues, I learnt later, described you as a queen-bee, another called you a slut. Someone even described that son-of-a bitch principal as your 'man'. I knew that you knew about all these comments but, stubborn as you are, you maintained a dignified indifference to demonstrate that you were not affected in the least by such offensive remarks. It was your way of saying that no one can hurt you in this way. Do you think such abominable gossips can actually inflict injury on anyone? Professional criminals can cause injury to a human body. People in our office were no less than criminals—only that they committed the crime of stealing the smile off one's lips and eyes, and that is not a punishable offence under any law.

They robbed you of everything that made you your true self. They forced you into a bleak, suffocating world of loneliness and detachment, where nothing cheerful ever happened. You lost everything a human being needs to live a normal life. They made you a cynic who distrusted and hated everyone, including yourself. Wasn't that enough to destroy you? What more harm could they have wrought upon you?

As I sit here helplessly watching you, that freak of a boss of yours keeps sneaking into my mind. My name for that creature was 'abortion', for I wished he had never been born. The man had a very limited vocabulary. The words he most used were 'I' and 'my'. He did not do anything constructive or fruitful in the present but would constantly narrate to you incidents of his past. Do you remember how many times and with what meticulous detail he told you of the lizard which entered his wife's vagina and how two doctors, two nurses, and he himself struggled to pull the reptile out? This was how he humoured himself—by having nothing to do with the present and by remaining concerned only with pulling the listener into his own past. The selfish bastard—there is no better word than 'abortion' for him.

Then there was that tragedy which befell his son in which he lost his leg in a train accident. The 'abortion' kept telling us how he himself had to go without food and spend sleepless nights for some weeks in the callous corridors of a Hyderabad hospital until the operation was complete. He never tired of mentioning that he spent almost two-and-a-half-lakh rupees on his son's treatment. He would tell the same stories again and again like a stuck gramophone. People such as your principal take great pride in concocting interesting tales out of such morbid events. They make their past the purpose of living in the present. Their reminiscences of the past supplies them the motive for their continued survival. Your principal would proudly narrate how his one-legged son has now joined a reputed company and how the company has insured the boy for twenty lakh rupees. His physically disabled son, the inept father boasts, has fetched him a fortune. Listening to his drivel, I secretly wished his wife would contract leprosy. By the time she would be cured, I thought, say in a year or so, she would have lost both her breasts and all her twenty fingers to the disease. Your principal, that 'abortion', would put his disfigured wife on exhibition. 'Look at her,' he would announce proudly. 'I have spent one lakh rupees to cure leprosy. She now has no breasts, no fingers, no disease!' Ha, isn't 'abortion' a most suitable name for him?

Lara, I can't imagine how anyone can stand such a man for even a few minutes. But you would spend a couple of hours each day with him. Predictably, I had made it a habit to return home alone. Even though you were unaware of them, you carried a load of despicable adjectives within you which only got heavier by the day. You were living within a cordon of enemies you yourself had involuntarily created. And I was your most intimate, your closest enemy. But you didn't know that.

You know, Lara, I detest God. I love gossip, I love to share jokes and play word games with people I like but I have never had any faith in or the slightest love for God. Yet, quite astonishingly, I came to believe in his existence just after you suffered the stroke. What a great sense of timing he has. He interfered at exactly the right moment and chose the right ailment for you, just as our relationship was about to be swallowed up by a bottomless whirlpool. Your epileptic stroke has rescued our fast-sinking 'relationship'.

You have now retired into a beautiful glasshouse and lie comfortably tucked away underneath a neat coverlet, oblivious to what goes on in the world around you. You have changed into a vegetable stored in a refrigerator, surrounded by the faint halo of an apparently permanent freshness. You are no longer a subject of salacious conversation among our colleagues. Your 'big boss' no longer gives me complexes, nor am I haunted by a sense of insecurity.

There would be so much love for me in those beautiful eyes of yours in the privacy of our home. But it was the condescending, commiserating look in your 'third eye' when we were in office that was used to dissolve my male arrogance. It made me feel so pathetically impotent. It made me understand how unproductive I was—I used to be constantly immersed in a miasma of frustration. Questions both pragmatic and profoundly philosophical—'Who am I?' 'Why am I alive in this world?' 'What do I contribute to society in lieu of the salary I draw every month?'—never stopped agitating me. I tried desperately to escape the torment. I once pulled off my sweater, threw it into the drain running along the office compound wall, and kicked it about. On three different days I destroyed three pens and cast the pieces away in different spots. On another occasion I slashed a couple of my shirts to shreds with a blade, used the pieces as rags to clean my motorbike, and threw them away. Does all this sound absurd? But that was how I vented my desperation. There were still more ways. I once stood fully dressed under the leaking overhead tank of our school and got drenched. On another occasion I hid in an unfrequented room in the office and spent the night there. Everyone frantically looked for me, I learnt later. I also heard that you spent the entire night worrying and weeping. The peon who unlocked the door the following morning was startled out of his wits to find me there.

Lara, you remember the day a group photograph of the teaching staff was taken? You stood beside that idiot, a cap upon your head and a broad smile on your face. That evening you made chicken for dinner—delicious! A strange thought crossed my mind as I ate. Suppose you had been butchered and diced and served in place of the chicken, would you taste as good? I believed that eaten in this way, one can completely merge the beloved's body into his own. The soul too—if there is one—mingles with the lover's soul in the same manner. Can there be a more convincing way to prove love? I have heard that Salvador Dali ate his pet rabbit in this manner. The creature's blood, flesh and marrow, its very soul, merged with his.

I am sure you know by now why I have come to believe in God. Hasn't he relieved me of my unbearable pain by choosing this particular ailment for you?

The doctor and the nurse told me only a few minutes ago that the medical board has consented to remove your life-support system. Do you know what that means? It means tomorrow will be curtains. Your time in the refrigerator will be at an end.

As for me, there will be no more pain, no more

aching realization of my own impotence. Tomorrow, I will be free of the illusions which have held me under a spell all these years. I will be detached from my 'self' and become a free soul. The stifling sense of inferiority, littleness and loneliness will disappear from the horizon of my consciousness. My heart is so overwhelmed with gratitude for God! And with such immense guilt that I haven't acknowledged his power until now.

Come to think of it, how insignificant is my existence compared to that of God. He is the formless Infinity, spreading endlessly across the cosmos, immense and all-pervasive. And, look, he has now chosen me as the 'blessed one' out of all the human beings who inhabit earth. Isn't that wonderful? I feel fully liberated. I am no longer trapped within the look of sympathy in my beloved wife's eyes, no longer pricked on all sides by the look of contempt in the eyes of the people around me. My entire being is flooded with such excitement and elation that I feel elevated almost to the level of God himself.

Lara, your secret pity, and the frank derision at school have reduced me to such a state that I was scared to face myself. But see how God has intervened in the right moment when I was about to sink into a labyrinth of terrible depression and self-loathing. Will you ever find such an act of benevolence in the pages of the history of mankind?

My salute to the life you live in the refrigerator!

~

Lara, I love you so very much! I love you! I love you! I love you!

Do you remember our early days? Our love flowered when you were at the very depths of a bottomless despair. Your elder brother had succumbed to cancer and you had been appointed in his place on compassionate grounds. You never smiled and almost every day I suggested that you must smile a little, just for a change. And when you smiled at long last, the smile first spread over your lips and travelled slowly to your eyes. You looked beautiful and your face glowed. It was I who reminded you to smile, you used to tell me, when you had long forgotten how to. 'Why do you love me so much?' you often asked. I would pinch you lightly in reply.

The memory of your first visit to my house is still vivid in my mind. You were startled by my caged snake. I took the snake out and asked you to touch it. You ran into the bedroom, screaming wildly. Amused, I flung the snake at your belly and you fainted. I sprinkled water on your face and you revived. But you were trembling like a leaf in a storm. You imposed a condition: 'The snake must go out of the house before our marriage.' The creature, however, conveniently died a few days later and our marriage was solemnized. Your parents, however, rightly guessed that it was I who was the snake and feared for your safety.

I did not want to marry. I did not conform to customs and had no faith in such social institutions. I accepted all suggestions and advice with apathetic resignation only to please you. I invited none of my friends or relatives to the marriage. I refused the customary marriage threads and the customary cork tiara. I asked the photographer not to take my pictures and fell asleep during the ceremony, shocking and surprising people beyond belief. No one dared to wake me up. It is possible—on that day a tiny seed of hatred was sown in some dark depths of my heart without my knowledge and, strangely enough, my love and loathing for you became synchronous. I have no idea when that seed germinated, became a sapling, and grew up into a poisonous tree. In the decade of our married life we loved and hated each other with equal intensity. We were like two teenagers, close friends who fight constantly yet long desperately for each other's company. We would talk for hours on end but there were also times when we had not one word to exchange with each other. Our love life sheltered beneath the shadow of the hate-tree. In a way, everything went smoothly until the day your friend joined as head of the institution. There came an immediate and sharp turn in the marriage we were both struggling to save. The poison-tree grew to its fullest size. Its dark, deadly shade so engulfed us that we lost sight of each other. And, surprisingly, the tree was uprooted that very day you suffered the stroke. You seemed to be far away from me as long as you were active and lively. But now that you lie in bed, unable to stand or speak or move, I feel you are intimately mine. There is no one in this world whom I possess more completely. What an irony.

We spoke over the phone for the first five hundred days of your stay in this cold chamber. You, of course, could not say anything; it was only I who talked the sweet nonsense I thought might bring you some relief from pain. You only smelled my words. Through the glass partition I anxiously watched the changes coming over your face, eyes and lips as I spoke. I tried hard to listen to the sounds of your laboured breathing, your feeble moans and, mostly, the sound of your undecipherable silences. Sometimes, when you cried softly, I cried, too. Something hard and gluey stuck at my throat when I watched the pain flash on your face. My stomach twisted and cramped, I felt breathless and my limbs froze. It was during those moments of bitter helplessness that I realized how precious you are to me. I understood how close we have become. You are no longer my closest enemy, you are the one closest to my heart. The poison-tree and its venomous shade have disappeared.

Lara, dear, would you like to know the contents of the submission I made to the medical board? In it, I wrote about a human being's right over his own life and death. I wrote about the meaninglessness of paying the huge price of one lakh rupees for loving you and seeing you alive and in pain. I asked them if it is ethically right to keep someone hanging hopelessly between life and death by artificial means. Is it right to let one wait endlessly at the mouth of a dark ice-cave for an angel which looks like a white bear? Who else but I myself am responsible for this body of mine? Who else has more right over my body and its pains but me? Which law enjoins me to keep spending money to live the life of a vegetable and to suffer unspeakable agony? There is no doubt that your family loves you a lot and does not want to let you die. But what about your suffering? Are you bound to continue bearing the pain of survival only so that they have a reason and a right to live? And, to view the matter from their perspective, why should they squander away all their resources and ignore every other emotion only to let you live like a vegetable? Which moral code can justify such a thing? If the law does not permit one to be released from this death-in-life, it is high time amendments were made to it so that it is made flexible in exceptional cases. Let the treatment be made time-bound and once that time passes, let no one be forced to drag on a life that has lost its beauty and appeal, a life turned worse than death.

A group of doctors and nurses came to me a few minutes earlier and informed me that the life-support system will be withdrawn at nine tomorrow morning. I inquired if it could be done earlier say, at seven. They refused and looked curiously at me. Thinking I had said something wrong, I said 'sorry', an apology in my voice. But the odd expression lingered in their eyes. I became a little unmindful after they left.

~

I woke up at six on the appointed day. I was feeling lightheaded and oddly relaxed. I looked at Lara. She lay as she had always lain over the last many days, her eyes fixed on nothing, her mouth half-open and slightly drooping. She looked—or was I just imagining it?—a little fresher than usual. The dozen tubes were still in place. The dots, lines, circles and half-circles, digits and letters still shone on the electronic screen. I have never looked at them or tried to understand them. But I tried to listen to the soft beeps of the computer, they sounded like music to my ears. I leisurely brushed my teeth and took a long shower, taking my time, hoping to relax. I picked out a tee-shirt and a pair of corduroy trousers from my briefcase and put them on. After placing an order for a cup of coffee I flopped into an armchair. Lara's parents arrived when I was halfway through my coffee. There were the inevitable lines of sleeplessness on their faces. Their eyes were red and swollen from long hours of weeping. They glanced disdainfully at me. I stood up and offered them a seat. Saying, 'I am coming,' I walked out into the corridor. I found twenty or so of our relatives there. They looked strangely at me when I wanted to know if anyone had met with an accident. It was still an hour before the magistrate arrived. The crowd bothered me. So I walked back to the doors of glass chamber that sheltered your shrunken form. A friend of mine and his wife stood there waiting for me, looking pale and drawn. A sympathetic hand touched my shoulder. I turned and smiled at my gloomy-faced friend. I offered him my hand. He seemed surprised and disapproving. Here I found another small group of our relatives. Each had a mournful look stamped upon his or her face. I should look as sad as them, I thought to myself. 'How much time it will take Lara to die after the tubes are removed?' I asked a nurse who stood near me. 'I can't say,' she answered uncertainly. 'In a minute maybe?' The group turned to look at me. I could discern a look of pity in their eyes. I wondered if I had become an object of pity. A few women stood around Lara's mother and spoke to her in hushed voices. Some were whimpering, the ends of their saris pressed to their faces.

One of my elder brothers had unexpectedly turned up. 'I have made all the arrangements for the funeral, you need not worry about that,' he said solicitously.

The thought of the funeral arrangements had somehow escaped my mind. But I was surprised all the same on seeing him there. We have not been on speaking terms for four years or so. Over the last thousand days he and my sister-in-law hardly paid us a visit in hospital. But I did not want to speak of those matters. 'There is no need,' I said shortly. 'There is an electric crematorium at the hospital which will take care of that.' All the others, including my elder brother, looked startled. I wondered again if I had said something wrong.

A man wearing a dhoti and a sacred thread on his shoulder came in and sat down cross-legged on the floor. Without bothering to ask anything to anyone he began intoning some unintelligible Sanskrit hymns in a singsong voice. I looked at the others. 'I have asked this priest to be here,' my elder brother said. 'He will chant some Vedic hymns for Lara.'

'Stop it,' I snapped. 'I won't have the last half-hour of Lara's life spoiled with this irritating noise.' To the priest, I said, 'Go away, please.' He looked up at me, astonishment in his eyes. 'Go, please,' I repeated myself. He rose to his feet and made way for the door, glaring at me.

The Superintendent of Police and the Collector arrived. I wondered who had asked them to be present. 'We are deeply sorry, Mr Das, take care,' the Collector said gently. 'It's all right.' I asked a ward boy to get coffee for them. Someone thanked me and said that I needn't bother. Lara's mother sobbed loudly. Everyone turned towards her. Some of our relatives took her out of the room.

At fifteen minutes to nine the Magistrate entered, accompanied by the Chief Medical Officer of the district along with four other doctors, an attorney, a couple of administrative staff of the hospital and a few others. A doctor went up to the electronic screen and noted the patient's temperature, heart rate and blood pressure. He also noted the percentage of damage to the brain. Then he lifted one eyelid, pulled out the tongue a little and examined it. He read the blood-, urine- and stool-test reports and made more notes. There was a thoughtful silence and, finally, he said: 'Over.' Every eye was fixed on my face. A photographer took two pictures and moved away. The atmosphere was thick with an almost-solid silence. No one said a word, no one moved. All eyes looked unblinkingly at Lara. Lara lay still, her vacant gaze fixed at an invisible point, her mouth slightly open. The sight seemed to have cleared out a blank space in the minds of those who stood watching. Another minute passed—a silence so heavy that, for the first time, I felt time has a weight of its own. I stood by her head. My hand stretched itself and touched her cheek tenderly. My lips moved but no sound emerged. The Magistrate peered at his watch and said, 'Okay.' The doctor came up to the bed and felt Lara's pulse. Another doctor disconnected all the twelve tubes one after another. That took two minutes. The computer ceased its beeping. A queer sound that resembled a stifled hiccup escaped Lara and in the next moment her head fell to one side. 'She is no more,' the doctor who stood feeling her pulse declared sombrely and let her hand fall. He walked up to the basin and washed his hand. The Magistrate left immediately. The nurse closed Lara's eyes and pulled a white sheet over her face. The medical officer placed a bouquet on Lara's chest. 'I am sorry, Mr Das,' he said, handing me an expense sheet which totalled sixty thousand rupees and went out. The Collector and the Superintendent of Police touched my shoulder, said, 'I am sorry,' and left too.

Lara's parents and others rushed inside as soon as the officials went out. As the crowd wailed I saw someone light a bunch of incense sticks and another spray perfume around the room. One of the women emptied a vermilion packet on Lara's forehead and the parting of her hair, and another sprinkled turmeric powder on her. A new sari was put upon her as were several garlands of flowers.

They put Lara on to a stretcher and led her to the crematorium. She was shifted to a steel plank projecting out of a huge machine. Lara slowly slid head-first into the giant, hollow machine. A switch was turned on and three minutes later a heap of smouldering ash slid out of the machine.

Just a few minutes earlier the steel plank which Lara had been laid on had looked so neat. She was here one minute and the next she had vanished. Metamorphosed into that ugly heap of ash as if by cruel magic. Lara is gone. Gone from the refrigerator, from this beautiful earth, from my life. Forever.

It took nearly five minutes for her ashes to cool down. Afterwards, someone held out a handful. 'Here she is, your Lara. Take her.' The agony stuck within me like an iceberg for one thousand days shattered without warning and drowned me in a flood of tears.

Pronunciation Therapy

'Sir, I am having "table" in my chest. I couldn't sleep all night.' An old lady, who didn't appear to be Odia, complained to Dr Haraprasad. Other patients waiting in the doctor's clinic looked curiously at the old woman. But the doctor seemed to have understood the woman's problem. He gestured to her that she should wait quietly and turned his attention to the patient he was examining.

'I am having "table" in my chest, sir,' the lady repeated. The doctor paid her no heed. 'Sir, I have tab—' the lady began.

'It is not "table"!' the doctor snapped. 'It is "trouble". I won't examine you as long as you keep pronouncing it incorrectly.' He looked in the other direction, vexed by the way the lady had mangled the word. That day, the doctor took nearly a couple of hours to teach the old lady the correct pronunciation of 'trouble', ignoring all the other patients. While he was lecturing the lady, some made their escape. They thought that they might further irritate the doctor by their incorrect pronunciation.

Dr Haraprasad was very touchy about the manner

in which patients spoke his name. Some called him 'Hariprasad' while others made it 'Haroprasad' or 'Haaraprasad'. He would be terribly upset when people mispronounced his name and had made it a principle to never treat such patients. The doctor, it was obvious, had a fetish for the correct pronunciation of words. 'People who cannot pronounce correctly lack character as well as confidence,' he used to say to his patients. 'It is because of this that our country is passing through a social and economic crisis. Correct pronunciation and the use of appropriate words at appropriate places will promote the economic growth of our country and help improve human relationships through healthier interaction.' Most of his patients, however, failed to understand how the correct pronunciation of words was connected to the economic prosperity of a country and better human relationships. But they preferred not to tax their brains much. After all, they were not students. They would rather worry about their sickness and their pain than the doctor's opinion on such complicated subjects.

At times, the doctor sometimes prescribed strange cures. A college student came to him complaining of terrible headache and joint pains which had lasted ten days. The doctor did not examine the patient. Instead, he wrote down something on a prescription and handed it over to the young man without saying a word.

It was at the chemist's shop that the student found—to his disappointment—that the doctor had not prescribed any drug. Instead, the prescription carried an advisory: the young man was to eat eggs and drink a glass of milk every day and regularly walk four kilometres. But the sheer absurdity and total unexpectedness of the advice worked a miraculous cure and the aches disappeared.

'Doctor, the increase in the size of my hydrogen is causing me a lot of trouble,' a patient complained. 'For the last one month I have been running a high temper—'

'Okay, okay.' The doctor cut in impatiently and scribbled something on a prescription. He handed the paper to the patient without a word. The man stared disbelievingly at its contents. 'A slight stirring in the patient's rising temper might explode his hydrogen and the ensuing deluge will drown our country. The patient, therefore, must immediately meet a great scientist; say, a person like Abdul Kalam, and seek his advice instead of coming to a doctor.' The patient looked on blankly. 'Get out,' the doctor said shrilly.

'You should have said hydrocele and temperature, not hydrogen and temper,' one of the patients sitting on the bench outside the doctor's chamber advised solicitously. But the doctor ignored the patient's entreaties and refused to examine him even after the man correctly pronounced the words.

In another such incident a patient described a boil as broiler and received similar treatment. 'Your broiler will grow to its full size in ten days,' the doctor jeered. 'Come to me then and I will get it operated. In the meantime get some onions, oil and spices to cook the broiler.'

The doctor was a few years above fifty, and his wife a little more than fifty-five. People said that while in college, the doctor was highly impressed by the perfectly accented pronunciation of a girl participating in a debate competition. After the event had ended he approached the girl and congratulated her. 'Your English is excellent...' the doctor said.

'Thanks.'

'Should I say that I have fallen in love with you and want you to be my wife?' the doctor, then a young student, ventured.

'Go to the dogs!' the girl snapped.

But young Haraprasad was not easy to brush off. Driven more by impulse than emotion, Haraprasad travelled two hundred kilometres to the town where the girl lived. Wasting no words, he said to the girl's parents that he would like to marry their daughter. Her parents were surprised by Haraprasad's straightforward approach and the unexpectedness of the proposal. The prospective groom was about five years younger than their daughter and they were not sure if society would view the match favourably. On the other hand, it was not easy to resist the temptation of having a doctor for a son-in-law. In the end, it took them just a week to make up their minds and agree to the match. The marriage was solemnized a month later. The girl sat beside the young doctor looking dazzling in her bridal finery. She smiled coyly at Haraprasad as his eyes caught hers.

It had never occurred to any one until Dr Haraprasad was married that correct pronunciation can play such a crucial role in match-making. And in the end, neither the doctor nor his family was disappointed. The bride conducted herself with perfect dignity; she dressed decently and possessed decorum in her manners. She proved to be a perfect choice and the doctor was more than satisfied with what life had to offer him.

The elder of his two daughters was in college while the younger was in school, completing her Higher Secondary. Both the girls seemed closer to their father than they were to their mother. Surprisingly, they sought their father's advice on everything, even in trifles like how they wore their hair, the newspaper they read, the menu of their meals, and the designs of dresses.

~

Sometime in the past the doctor had visited a patient in a village inhabited mostly by tribal people. The patient turned out to be the wizened old man Duaru, who was regarded with great reverence by the village folk because of his supernatural powers. Every year in the month of Chaitra, the spirit of the village God would possess Duaru and the old man, possessed by a supernatural force, would roam about the villages, hissing and puffing like some otherworldly creature. A black loincloth would be wound around his waist, his forehead would be smeared with vermilion, and his long matted hair would hang loose as the old man ran wildly along the village streets, his anklets jingling. The villagers would give way to him in awe, standing with folded palms even as he sped past them brandishing a tamarind-tree cane in one hand and a bunch of peacock plumes in the other. He would predict the future in an unintelligible language—which people believed was spoken by the gods—and lash at the people with the cane. A rope-swing hung from the branches of a large tamarind tree on the outskirts of the village. A small wooden board tied to the ropes served as a seat. However, shockingly, several iron spikes were fixed to the seat and the old man, seated on the spiked seat, would rock to and fro and offer his blessings to the crowd which would have gathered from his own village and other villages in the vicinity. The air would reverberate with the blowing of conches, the beating of cymbals and drums, and the ululations of women-folk.

It so happened that the doctor had taken his younger daughter along with him to that village. He wanted her to correct people if they used inappropriate words or pronounced them wrongly. The rope-swing on the outskirts of the village caught the girl's interest. She walked up to the swing but the spike-studded seat made her pause. But the doctor encouraged her to try to sit on the board, to at least see what sitting on spikes felt like, and thus inspired, the girl began to swing. People gathered, in ones and twos at first and then in greater numbers until a crowd had gathered. 'That swing is for our God only,' they warned the doctor.

'If anyone other than our God sits on it, the spirit of the God enters that person and kills him.' They could not protest strongly, though, for fear of displeasing the doctor. Incidentally, the girl suffered from a fever for a few days after the incident and the village-folk were certain that the fever was God's punishment. But the girl was soon cured.

After that incident two unexpected things happened. Old Man Duaru, the awe-inspiring God-incarnate, who had been confined to his sick bed for quite some time, broke down in helpless tears. 'Doctor Harryprasad is my God,' he declared to his mother. 'Only he can relieve me of this pain and suffering.' (Luckily, the doctor had not heard the way Duaru pronounced his name, or he would never have treated the old man and the 'God' would have been left to his fate.)

The village folk, too, appeared to have become a little skeptical about Old Man Duaru's omnipotence. It had never crossed their imagination that anyone other than Duaru could sit on the rope-swing and survive their God's wrath. But after the doctor's daughter sat on the swing some naughty children of the village followed her example. The more mischievous ones among them even plucked out many of the spikes from the board. The parents, too, no longer stopped their kids from making such mischief. Most of the villagers appeared to have gotten over their fear of Old Man Duaru. They no longer revered him and called him a fraud to his face. A few days later the swing itself disappeared from the tamarind tree. 'The God has stolen it for himself,' the village people remarked even as they laughed scornfully.

~

One day, in the grey light of dawn, someone saw a shadowy figure jumping over the wall which guarded the doctor's compound. The figure moved unsteadily across the lawn towards the back of the house. 'A thief has sneaked into the doctor's house,' he said anxiously to another and the news travelled all over the locality in no time. In no time a curious crowd gathered in front of the main gate of the doctor's house. A couple of policemen on night patrol too lumbered up. They tried to wake the doctor and tell him about the thief. It took them nearly one hour. By the time the doctor got up and learned about the incident it was time for sunrise. The doctor opened the back door of his house and found a man sitting hunched over. The doctor walked up to the man and looked closely. Old Man Duaru, pale and drawn, burning with fever, looked up imploringly at the doctor. The doctor took Duaru's bony hand and helped him up. 'Come with me,' he said.

The doctor and Old Man Duaru walked along the alleyway that looped past the doctor's house and up to the main door. The doctor sent word inside for the keys to the main gate and his clinic. He motioned the people outside the gate to keep quiet and, opening the main gate, walked along the garden path leading to his clinic, taking Duaru along.

The crowd in front of the doctor's house had grown larger by that time. It comprised old men on their morning walks, young joggers, women on their way to the temple, elderly men just out of bed and with toothbrushes in hand, and some daily labourers walking to construction sites. There were a few curious rickshaw-pullers and beggars too. Everyone loudly speculated and readied themselves to give the man the treatment he deserved. The two night-patrol policemen were all geared up to drag Duaru to the police station.

Contradicting everyone, the doctor entered his clinic, holding Duara by the hand, and pulled the shutter down behind him even as everyone looked on in surprise.

By that time the news of a thief stealing into the doctor's house had invaded most houses of the locality like unobstructed sunlight. The matter had been reported to the nearest police station, too. The phone inside the doctor's house, after ringing several times, had finally fallen silent. But the shutter of the clinic remained resolutely shut.

One hour passed, and then another two—the clinic did not open nor did the doctor or the man emerge.

By the end of three suspenseful hours the growing impatience of the crowd was getting a little difficult to keep under control. The small whispers had given way to a loud buzzing and everyone now seemed to be more interested in freeing the thief from the doctor's clutches.

The door finally opened and the doctor came out, a cup of tea in hand. 'The old man died,' he said to the first person he met. Everyone stood stunned, as though hit by a thunderbolt. The old man, the villagers knew, was none other than their 'God' Duaru, and they couldn't be sure if they could believe the doctor. But nobody could muster confidence to ask the doctor what exactly had happened.

The post-mortem report arrived later during the day and the truth came to light, too. Old Man Duaru had been suffering from pneumonia. The doctor had made all efforts to save his life. He had even administered a life-saving drug as a last resort but had not been able to save Duaru. It was only a few months earlier that the doctor had treated Duaru and cured him.

Duaru's wife had died many years earlier and he lived with his old mother. Duaru had great respect for Dr Haraprasad. 'He is my God,' he was fond of saying. His mother had succumbed to pneumonia a few days earlier. Duaru had himself suffered high fever after having performed the funeral rites for his mother. And, driven by an irrepressible desire to meet his God and pay him his respects, the old man had walked all the way up to the doctor's house in the town in the middle of the night.

A Picture of Agony

RUSHI STOOD BEFORE the wall and talked to her father who smiled at her from behind the glass.

'Do you know, Father, the temperature here has touched 45°C today. It was three years ago, on a scorching day like this, that you, Ma and Grandma left this world. For the last two years Grandpa and I have been observing a 45°C day as your death anniversary. It was on such a day that sunstroke invaded our lives. Burning, scalding 45°C—like today. Grandpa has gone to town to get fruit. Didn't Ma and you relish fruit salad? That is why Grandpa came up with the idea of offering fruit salad to passersby. You know, Father, Grandpa doesn't listen to me nowadays. He did not wrap a wet cloth around his head, nor did he carry an umbrella with him. He argued with me, and scolded the sun. You could have asked him to be more careful had you been here.' Rushi stopped talking to her father and drank some water. Then she lay down on the bed and gazed at her mother for a long time who hung beside her father and looked fondly at her. She drifted off to sleep.

'Rushi, get up now,' Grandpa called out. She looked at the clock. She had slept for nearly an hour. Rushi and her grandfather now diced the fruits—the papayas, watermelons, apples, bananas, and pomegranates. They added sugar and cream to the fruit mix and put them in about two hundred disposable plastic cups. They then carried the cups to the field that stretched beyond the back of their house and arranged them neatly on the three graves there.

Rushi's mother used to teach in a primary school five kilometres from their house. She used to cycle to and from the school. In summer, the school started in the morning and wound up by noon. That day she came home at twelve and, all at once, her head began to reel and she died. 'It is sunstroke,' the doctor declared. 'We will cremate her in the field behind the compound wall,' Father said. Rushi and Grandpa agreed. Just three days later, Grandma's funeral rites too were performed in the same field, about a hundred metres or so from the house. 'She had sunstroke,' Father said and wept for long hours. Grandpa comforted him and wiped his tears with the border of the sari wrapped around Grandma's dead body. Both Father and Grandpa had their heads tonsured and their moustaches and beards shaved. They decided to construct graves with brick and cement and fix an epitaph to each. Two masons worked under Father's supervision and built three platforms, each four feet long, two feet wide and two feet high. They worked hard and completed the work in two weeks. The names of Rushi's mother and grandmother were artistically inscribed on plates fixed to their respective tombs. The dates of their deaths, too, were inscribed. 'Let it be mentioned that 45°C was the cause of their death,' Rushi suggested. Accordingly, the cause of their death was also mentioned. The masons went away after receiving their payment. Father came home and asked for some water. He died just as he was drinking a glass of water.

Rushi had no idea if such chaos had ever invaded any one's life. Her brain seemed to have become paralyzed. She could not think, she could not weep. The girl and her grandfather sat motionless for nearly an hour, away from each other, as if one would become defiled by the touch of the other. No sound seemed to enter their ears; neither footsteps, nor the jingle of bangles, not even the voices of people who stood close to them. They had all been turned to wood. They must weep, relatives and the neighbours thought. They tried to open Rushi's and her grandfather's clenched jaws and force them to drink some water. They splashed water on their faces. Someone made Rushi sit on her grandfather's lap. Another brought out a photograph of Ma and showed it to Rushi. Someone else held Grandma's photograph before her grandfather's eyes. Slowly, after a long time, Rushi and her grandfather sensed each other's presence—only through touch—and each of them wept a little.

Rushi wanted to weep some more but couldn't. The

heat of the sun had dried her tears. It had also scorched
her life. Ruthless, heartless sun! Rushi tried to judge the
sun's capacity to burn. It can scorch the earth, the air
and the water too, she thought bitterly. It can also char
emotions. It can burn away all trust and happiness. But
the sun could never burn her agony away, Rushi was sure
of that. 'My agony is private, the heat of the sun cannot
reach it. There is a yawning gap between my agony and I.
The sun cannot scan the space which separates me from
my grief. What does the sun think of itself? There is a
limit to the extent to which it can exercise its power. It
can never trespass on my agony despite all its strength.
Why, then, do people perform the Surya Namaskar?' A
vengeful satisfaction swept over Rushi when she realized
that her raging pain could defeat the sun.

Grandpa kept assuring Rushi that he would not fall
victim to sunstroke until the temperature reached 48°C.
This assurance boosted her confidence and made her
happy. It helped her sustain the pain and measure the
distance between herself and her agony.

The picture of Rushi and her agony appeared in
a newspaper the day after her father died. Below the
picture was a news item: 'Three members of a single
family have succumbed to sunstroke. The government
is trying to evade its duty. It did not announce any ex-
gratia payment for the family. The government will be
held responsible for the consequences...' People from
the media interviewed Rushi's grandfather. Grandfather

spoke into a microphone and cast aspersions on the sun:
'Does the sun have a right to maraud us in this manner
just because we hold it as the source of all energy? Can
it exercise its wilfulness on us without any restriction?
Its arrogance must be challenged. Its freedom to abuse
its power must be curbed. Let the sun be henceforth
declared a dictator, a tyrant, a killer. Let the practice of
the Surya Namaskar be omitted from the curricula of
Yoga schools. We condemn, we condemn… the unruly,
unjust sun. Down, down! The killer sun… Down, down!'
Grandfather said. Others shouted slogans against an
oppressive sun and an unfair government.

The previous year, a new road had been constructed
under the Prime Minister's Rural Road Development
Scheme, which passed by the patch of unused land
behind Rushi's house where the three graves stood. It
was a busy road for most of the day as it connected two
highways. Vehicles of all sorts, light four-wheelers as
well as heavy trucks with sixteen and twenty-two wheels
plied all day.

Now Rushi's grandfather and their well-wishers tried
to work out a plan to put the patch of land to some use.
Rushi's father's colleagues at the fire station where he
had worked suggested that either a hotel could be set up
there or a shop that would sell betel, cigarettes and other
tobacco products. 'No,' said Rushi. 'No,' her grandfather
said firmly. Any business remotely linked with heat and
fire was to be strictly ruled out. No one must light a match

or an oven. Father, Ma and Grandmother cannot bear heat, they said. They would rather set up a parlour which vended something cold, like ice cream, or lemonade, or fruit juice. And plans were accordingly made. Rushi and her grandfather salvaged whatever they could from her parents' savings and constructed a large air-conditioned hall. The three graves stood in the middle of it. The doors and windows were fitted with glass panels. New brocaded curtains were hung. A refrigerator and an electronic mixer-grinder, glasses and cups, and chairs were bought. The three graves were fitted with marble toppings. The obscenities which some wicked boys had scratched on the grave were polished clean. Chairs were placed around the three graves and the ice-creams, the cool fruit juice and the cool lemonade were put on their marble tops. Father, Mother and Grandma now stayed in peace in the air-conditioned room. They were safe, out of the reach of the tyrant sun and its fatal heat.

~

The temperature is 45°C today. So Rushi and her grandfather will observe this day as the death anniversary of Rushi's father, her mother, and her grandmother. They will offer fruit salads to people free of cost, to the bare-bodied urchins who run and play all through the noon, braving the heat, the truck-drivers on the road, the office staff of the fire station, housewives, the woodcutter, the newspaper-hawker, the schoolmistress who walks along carrying an umbrella, and many others. Rushi and her grandfather promise their sorrow a private appointment sometime later and wear a look of happiness over their faces. Today is a day of celebration, a day to take shelter from the furnace of gloom and eat iced fruit salads in the company of people.

'What a jovial character Father was!' Rushi reminisced. 'A good-natured man with a heart surging with dreams!'

'We will escape to the North Pole if the temperature crosses 45°C this summer,' Rushi used to tell her father. 'To Norway maybe—the land which has six months of uninterrupted day and six months of uninterrupted night. Won't it be fun?'

'Yes, we will do that. Start packing now,' her father would say pleasantly. 'Do you know what happens when the sun never sets for six months? You know how the two ends of the rainbow seem to connect the east and the west? The sun keeps moving to and fro along a similar trajectory. For six consecutive months the sun comes up in the eastern horizon at six in the morning and in the next twelve hours it keeps travelling from east to west, and then again from the west to the east along this rainbow-like route. That is why the sun appears again in the eastern horizon exactly after twelve hours, and there is another "six o'clock in the morning" after twelve hours. This is the reason why there is never a "six o'clock in the evening" during those months. The sun rises twice every day. Two mornings every day—how divine! A heavenly land of ice basks in the soft beams of a kind, humble sun! One could fall in love with the sun there. But here, we repel the sun. We despise the Surya Namaskar!'

Rushi would bubble with excitement. 'We will build an ice-house. I have read that the temperature there always remains between 0 and -30°C. We can use cookware made of ice, furniture made out of ice—bowls and glasses and cooking pots, tables and chairs of ice. Everything there is cool, everything is gentle and soft. The sun is a loving sun there, caring and caressing. No one suffers from sunstroke. Instead, its gentle warmth enchants and rejuvenates. We will spend summer in that land of ice, Father. We will spend summer in the polar belt. This sun can't bring us any harm there. The sun that rises there is a different sun.'

As Rushi planned a summer vacation in the North Pole, the temperature kept rising, from 45 to 46, 47 to 48°C. It then climbed down to 41°C and still lower until, finally, the summer vacation was at an end.

~

It was another hot day on another summer vacation. The temperature was 44°C.

'Rushi, come and see what I have here,' her mother called out excitedly.

'What's it, Ma?'

'Look at this soap-wrapper. We have won a lottery. It says that Aishwarya Rai and Abhishek Bachchan will visit our house.' The news electrified the neighbourhood and spread far and wide in that small town in no time. The telephone rang non-stop. There was continuous knocking at the door. At every little sound the heart skipped a beat. The dogs barked always, or would it be more appropriate to say, the dogs *laughed* always? The trees looked lush green despite the heat. The cats, the sparrows, the pigeons and the parrots became restless with excitement. A tsunami came. Huge tides swelled in the ocean. The air felt cold to the touch. An icy coolness seemed to have settled over the houses and the courtyards. The earth and the sands stopped becoming hot. The heat of the sun weakened. The cooling cucumber-and-curd salad was no longer in demand. People no longer needed sunglasses. No one remembered the sun and the sun, like a truant fleeing school, sneaked out of the lives of the people of that small town. Rushi, her family, and their neighbours began sweeping their courtyards. They washed the walls and the doors of their houses clean with soap-water and swabbed their floors with antiseptic-fortified water. They hung new curtains and changed the bedspreads. They flushed their alimentary canals from the mouth at one end to its furthest extremity with thousands of litres of water and lemon juice. No one bothered that the prices of lemon and salt kept rising. Rushi said, 'Father, we must get an expensive settee which will reflect our aesthetic taste and our culture.' One day she brought home her friends and said, 'Father, all my friends have bought new dresses for the occasion. I will have to, too.' Another day, she asked, 'Father, they are celebrities. What kind of snacks should we offer them? What would they prefer to drink? Tea, coffee or sherbet?'

'They are stars,' her father said. 'Stars don't eat what the common man does: rice, bread, salt, pickles. They eat time and space, rivers, canals, jungles and hills. They drink moon beams and the ocean. The sound of their snoring creates cracks in mountains. There are explosions in the solar system when stars yawn. When their feet fall on the ground, there are upheavals in the nation's economy. It is for them that Dalal Street trembles.'

'My friend has volunteered to lend us their air-conditioner for that day. We will install it in our living room,' Rushi said to her father. 'We will enjoy the cold air. How lovely!'

'The news of the visit has blunted the edge of the heat,' Father said. 'The temperature seems to have come down to 30°C. I think it will come down by ten degrees more when they arrive.' Of course, how they dress would determine whether the heat will go up or come down. For some, the temperature might shoot up to 50°C. Some might get exceedingly emotional and lose consciousness. Any number of unexpected incidents might happen. Everything could go berserk. Even the dogs may get too excited and run about attacking innocent people.

Summer vacation was about to end. It was the time for the schools and colleges to reopen. Yet the stars didn't come, and the date of their arrival kept being postponed, like a lotus drifting away from a swimmer reaching out to pluck it until, one day, it was finally announced that the stars wouldn't be coming at all. They gave several sensible reasons: the town didn't have an airstrip for their plane to land; there was no five-star hotel in town where they could stay; the town did not figure either on either a geographical or a political map; it did not have a history of its own nor was it economically sound.

This town thrives only on dreams, on empty promises, the sun and its burning heat, it was said. The government is incapable of taking adequate measures to block out the sun, nor does it have the moral courage to challenge it. The lotus will never bloom here. The soap which declares prizes on its wrapper will henceforth be banned in this town.

~

Rushi has lived life at its lowest ebb these last three years. Initially, a black despair had swept all her emotions away, leaving her empty. But now she treasures her agony. She has collected clippings of her broken, woebegone face which had appeared on newspaper pages, framed them, and hung them on the wall. She looks at her pictures and says to herself, 'That me in the photo is not me. I could never be the epitome of agony like she is.' She says the same thing to her grandfather: 'I am not Agony, I am different.' Alongside the newspaper clippings she has also hung framed photographs of other weeping girls, all of whom look pathetic and miserable. Rushi looks on at those pictures of agony and intones, 'I am not Agony, I am different. All of Agony is hanging on that wall.'

She used to play a game of snakes-and-ladders with her agony. At times the snake would swallow her and she would slide back into the depths of despair. At other times, she would climb a ladder and reach high. And looking down from her perch she would see Agony sniveling and groveling at the tail of the snake. There were times when her body would become hard, solid, and acquire a well-defined shape. At times it would become smoky and blurred, amorphous and centreless. She would wonder what she could with a body that had changed into a sticky, pulpy, slippery lump of clay and begin to mould it back into its regular shape. She would try to give her deranged, disfigured life a definite shape, a specific direction, a point of view, fresh meaning. She would stand in front of the photos of her parents and her grandmother, choosing a position from where she knew her grandfather could hear her, and say, 'Ma, I will go to the park today. I will get balloons, toys, ice cream and a new dress. I will also get coloured light-bulbs to decorate the soft-drink parlour.'

That day, all the naked kids who came to the parlour were made to sit in the air-conditioned hall. She gave them fruit salad. People kept coming in all afternoon. Wayfarers, bikers, cyclists, cart-pullers, jeep and truck drivers—everyone came in to the parlour to get a free serving of fruit salad. No one discussed the temperature. But a truck-driver mentioned that it had risen from 45 to 46°C. Rushi tried to ignore that, but her heart skipped a beat. She forced herself to concentrate on serving fruit salad to new arrivals, her heart thumping.

When the parlour had newly opened, mothers had warned their children not to visit. They frightened the kids away saying that the place was haunted. But since the previous year, after Rushi had started distributing fruit salad on the 45°C days, they ignored all warnings and kept gathering around Rushi and asking for chocolates and balloons.

In the evening Rushi went to the market on her scooter. She bought chocolates, toys and ice cream for the customers, and coloured light bulbs to decorate the parlour. She stood before her parents who smiled at her from the wall and said, 'You will see, Father, how lovely the parlour will look tomorrow. I will decorate it myself. But Father, I must tell you that Grandpa doesn't listen to me these days. He doesn't take any precautions against the heat. At times he forgets his umbrella and he doesn't take medicines regularly. Nor does he drink sufficient quantities of lemon and salt water. But he keeps forcing me to eat more.'

Grandfather came up to Rushi and said, 'Rushi, Rushi, my child, my darling, aren't you going a little too far? Today I had my umbrella with me when I went to the market. I did drink lemon and salt water, and took my medicine, too. Not good, not good baby!'

'I am sorry, Grandpa,' Rushi said apologetically and smiled. Rushi couldn't think of anyone other than the sun as her dearest arch enemy. Who else could she think of challenging, if at all? The sun had made her shed so many tears that she had metamorphosed into a sticky lump of clay. But she had decided that this was the right time to give her life a regular and well-defined shape. The photographer's camera had captured the image of her grief-stricken face and held it still. He had immortalized the agony her body was writhing under. The picture of agony on the photograph will not change. But Rushi is a human being, and a human being changes every moment. The creases of pain on Rushi's face which the camera holds out may be an inspiration for those who can notice it. The picture of agony may move a poet to write a poem, a painter to make a portrait, or a sculptor to chisel an image in stone. But Rushi cannot see the lines of pain, nor can she identify herself with the picture of agony that the camera has captured. The agony caught in the photograph is hard, solid and impenetrable. It is not subject to change. 'But the agony I am experiencing is not the same. There is a difference, almost of heaven and hell, between the pain that the photo has defined and the real agony I am experiencing. I can never be an embodiment of pain. I am different. If I am to be compelled to experience the agony depicted in the picture, may the sun permanently imprison me in a crucible of heat. Let it make me the epitome of agony. But it does not possess the power to bring me and the agony I am passing through together. It cannot make the two separate levels of my existence merge. Only I own that power of discretion. It is only I who can decide if I shall let it happen.'

The following day, grandfather and granddaughter worked together and decorated the parlour with coloured light-bulbs, flowers, balloons, tiny artificial butterflies. The parlour looked beautiful. Rushi, too, looked beautiful. There was a gleam in her eyes and a smile on her lips.

Towards the latter part of the evening Grandfather looked pale and tired. Rushi asked a truck-driver, a stranger, who had come to the parlour what the temperature was on that day. 'Forty-seven degrees Celsius,' the man said. Rushi, all smiles, turned to her grandfather and said delicately, 'Grandpa, the temperature today is forty-seven degrees Celsius.'

By then, Rushi's grandfather had collapsed and died.

Sentenced to a Honeymoon

NACHIKETA WAS AN odd sort of a fellow, an eccentric. Sleeping inside a mosquito-net made him uneasy. A dip in water suffocated him. The smell of incense made him feel as if he was trapped in fragrant mist. He felt claustrophobic in a closed bathroom. He would get upset if the doors of his study were left open. His wife's company for more than a certain number of hours agitated him. Writing letters to loved ones puzzled him.

One night, Nachiketa disappeared. When his wife Deepa woke in the morning she found his bed empty. The door was wide open, as were the windows. Perhaps he has gone for his morning walk, she thought, and did not pay his absence more heed. When he did not return at his usual time she thought he must be with a friend, but felt a slight uneasiness, and a few more hours passed. Nachiketa did not show up.

As the hours went by, the futile waiting dissolved into a chaos of hope, doubt, debate, solace, solicitousness, assurance and panic. By evening there was frantic despair, fear, tears, hunger and thirst, and the blaring of at least a hundred cellphones.

Nachiketa had left his cellphone behind and his ringtone was that of a mewing kitten. The kitten mewed, remained silent for a while, and began mewing again. This went on for five days until the cellphone battery discharged.

Nachiketa's disappearance remained shrouded in mystery. Somebody said that Nachiketa had bought thirty envelopes from the post office the previous day. All the thirty envelopes will be posted to one address, one on each day, he had said. They kept guessing and looking for the possible address Nachiketa intended to send the letters to, but without any success.

It took two days for Nachiketa's wife to find Tooty's phone number. (Tooty was one of Nachiketa's former flames.) Deepa and Tooty had fought bitterly over Nachiketa years earlier. But Deepa was now compelled to call Tooty and inquire about Nachiketa's whereabouts. However, Tooty was genuinely surprised to learn that Nachiketa was missing. She sounded extremely humble and shy yet reasonably convincing when she told Deepa that she had no idea where Nachiketa was. Deepa was, however, not completely convinced. Some of her friends and relatives wanted to know who this Tooty was, but tight-lipped taciturnity was the only reply they received from Deepa.

Days after Nachiketa's disappearance Deepa received a summons from the district court where she was asked to personally appear on a scheduled date. The identity of the mysterious addressee of the thirty envelopes was finally revealed. All of the letters had been addressed to the district judge who, more out of curiosity than exasperation, had decided to look into the matter.

Both Deepa and Nachiketa reached the court on the appointed date and stood in the two witness docks facing each other. Deepa wore her shampooed hair in a topknot. Clad in a polka-dotted, coffee-coloured sari with a slim border, its plaits held in place in neat folds, she looked presentable and fresh. Nachiketa looked grubby; his beard was unkempt, his fingernails unclipped and his clothes shabby. He smiled a small smile at Deepa.

The judge was ushered into the courtroom.

'Let your wife know about your complaints,' said the judge to Nachiketa without preamble.

'I have already mentioned everything in my letters to you, my lord,' Nachiketa replied.

'Your wife knows nothing of those matters. I myself have noted a few points but, first, I want you to precisely explain your position to the Court. And before anything, tell the Court why your wife thinks of you as a person who does not live a disciplined life.'

Nachiketa began, 'Your honour, my wife never stops reminding me how disciplined our neighbour Mr Vishwavasu is. He lives by a strict routine, and all his activities are set to it. He gets up exactly at nine in the morning, begins drinking tea at nine-five and, at nine-fifteen, goes out to get vegetables. He takes a bath at nine-thirty, puts on his underwear at nine-forty and the rest of his clothes five minutes after. He eats breakfast at nine-fifty, wheels his scooter out at nine fifty-five. At nine fifty-seven he wipes the dust off the seat and starts for the bank exactly a minute later. One can set time on one's watch by Mr Vishwavasu's routine. Day in and day out, my wife accuses me of my inability to emulate the regularity and disciplined lifestyle of this neighbour of ours.'

The judge looked at Deepa. 'Do you have anything to say?'

'Let him first respond,' Deepa said.

Nachiketa began again, a derisive smile on his lips. 'So Mr Vishwavasu—an epitome of discipline! But I ask... Does this epitome of discipline adjust his coughing and sneezing to clock time? At what clock time does he yawn and for how many seconds does he keep his mouth open? At what clock time does a moonlit night exalt him? At what clock time does he enjoy the sight of a sparrow dipping in a pool of water, or a bird weaving its nest? For how many exact minutes or hours does he gaze at stars in a clear night sky? At what time of the day does he watch a pheasant pick at a snail? Does he keep a record of the exact time the flowerbud on his plant opens its petals? How can time be measured with such exactitude? The truth is that Time and the clock are not the one and same thing. A clock cannot define Time.'

Nachiketa paused and looked at the judge, an intense

look of appeal in his eyes. The judge averted his gaze and moved on to the next point.

'Mr Nachiketa, you have also mentioned your wife's complaint that you are an incompetent householder. The Court would like you to be more explicit in this matter.'

'Your Honour, my wife holds a high opinion of Mr Vishwamitra, one of my friends, as an efficient and responsible householder. Mr Vishwamitra faces no difficulty in obtaining cooking-gas cylinders, or the controlled rations which are due to us from the dealer. Mr Vishwamitra can manage to get anything with the least effort: be it sugar, wheat or petrol—items which are scarcely available in the market for people like me. Electricians, plumbers and the deliverymen who bring the cooking-gas cylinders home find me easy prey. But Mr Vishwamitra is nobody's fool. My wife judges my competence as a householder by these yardsticks.'

'Isn't it a fact that I am being put to a lot of trouble because of this?' Deepa interjected.

Nachiketa continued, without looking at his wife, 'When the competent Mr Vishwamitra walks home at night, the strays bark. They hate him. But when they see me coming they yip and wag their tails. They know I will have biscuits with me. When I crush an insect on a wall lizards rush in from four directions. The first lizard gets the prey but the rest look at me, a question in their eyes: "Where is my share?"'

'What do you feel your wife thinks of your social status?' the judge asked when Nachiketa stopped.

'I am a misfit in the society we live in. That's what she thinks.' Nachiketa paused and looked around the courtroom. 'She cites the example of Mr Vashistha, a respectable person by her standards. Mr Vashistha, according to her, draws a lot of water in town. He can manoeuvre things to suit his purpose. He can obtain access to an intellectual gathering and can wrangle passes for operas and other such programmes meant exclusively for the elite. He can manage discounts on refrigerators, air-coolers, a motorbike, jewellery or saris. Bricks, cement, chicken, fish—nothing is beyond Mr Vashistha's easy reach. I don't enjoy such social privilege. I have to stand in a queue and wait my turn. In my wife's eyes, I am an also-ran in a society of worthies such as Mr Vashistha.'

'Haven't there been times when "not being like Mr. Vashistha" has put us in a lot of trouble?' Deepa countered.

'To tell you the truth, Your Honour,' Nachiketa carried on, ignoring Deepa's remark, 'I enjoy prestige in my flower-garden. Every time I walk in, a flower blooms and a leaf changes colour to welcome me. I can see through binoculars the grasshopper which sits still among thick shrubs like a hermit in meditation. To greet me, a weaver-bird illuminates its nest with a glow-worm it has carefully picked. Tiny flowers of the shefali tree hang loosely on branches, ready to fall into my palms as I walk underneath it in dewy dawns. A soft smile flutters on their petals when I hold them tenderly in my palms.'

The judge moved on to the next point. 'What are her complaints regarding your health?'

'On matters of good health, my wife is a great admirer of my friend Mr Sandipani. He is tall and muscularly built, and has a shock of thick glossy hair which enhances his looks. I look shoddy by his side, with an ill-shaped body like a farm labourer—as my wife is fond of reminding me time and again. Mr Sandipani is extremely health conscious and my wife likes him for that. He never goes out in the rain and stays at home to avoid the sun. In the cold months he wears a sweater, wraps a muffler around his head, and wears a filter-mask before leaving home. I never care to adopt such safety measures to protect my health despite her continual warnings. She probably has no idea that storm or rain or lightning or thunder have no control over me. Cold, heat, light, darkness cannot influence me in any manner. Nor can I control them. On their own they may be soft, intense, fierce and furious but cannot touch a self that is placid, dispassionate and detached.'

The judge glanced at Deepa. She was wiping her face, perhaps her tears. She did not say a word.

'Does your wife think of you as a conscientious character? Does she merit your intellect and regard you as a knowledgeable man?'

'As far as creative writing goes, my wife holds my friends Mr Vyashadev and Mr Valmiki in high esteem. In her opinion their writings have felicity of expression and a fluid style whereas I am inarticulate. What I write is complex, obscure and vitriolic. One rarely likes to read about the repulsive things my writings abound in: rickety bullocks, death, bluebottle flies. I think she is a little confused and unsure about what she exactly expects me to do. When I quit writing for a few days and while my time away in idle gossip with Vyashadev and Valmiki she cannot accept it as normal. "Why aren't you writing these days?" she frets. But when I return to my desk she taunts, "You wear such a pathetic look when you write, as if some terrorist is holding you hostage." At other times she complains, "You make me feel absolutely unwanted when you write." She is occasionally concerned that for me writing is a painful exercise, a deadly, bloody battle with intransigent words. She then tells me, "Forget about writing if it hurts you so much.'"

Nachiketa paused briefly, and resumed, 'She is right in a way. As I sit at my table a mob of words is released willy-nilly from within the pages of books, mythologies and dictionaries; from within the innermost being of culture itself. They writhe all over the room, hissing like snakes, their lethal fangs poised to strike. Unruly words maraud the room and trample all over the table, the chairs, the bookcase. The furniture dissolves; the books melt in a venomous heat and slither out of the shelves. The room becomes a bedlam, bursts with the thunder of boulders hurtling down mountains, the galloping of horse hooves, the deafening roar of an angry ocean. It feels like a tornado's assault. Words, syntaxes, punctuation and numbers whirl about. Then they come crashing down with untold violence and smash into me. It is with superhuman effort that I confront them, placate them and hold them in place. And, eventually, they calm down and surrender. That experience is like the absolute joy of consummation. Yet the act fills my wife with such abhorrence that she vomits.'

The judge found that he was sweating and mopped his face with a handkerchief. He looked up to make sure that the fan was working.

'Do your dreams and your impulses frazzle her? Does she have any complaints there?'

Nachiketa said, sounding amused, 'A lot. In fact there were several incidents which she found puzzling. For instance, one time, I confined myself in the house for several days, having locked the door from the outside. I lie in the bathtub for hours, reading a book. At times I fall asleep in an open field on chilly winter nights. I once spent an entire week in a lonely bungalow on Gandhamardan hill. Then there was that incident when I slept on a park bench all night. I had gone to her parental home to attend her father's funeral rites, but left without telling anyone. My wife was scared out of her senses when I brought home a human skeleton from the school laboratory and kept it in the living room as an article of decoration for a couple of days. She couldn't sleep on those two nights and the entire week which followed.

I have left her in the market and in many other places in town and driven back home thinking she is sitting behind me on the scooter. She has always complained about how I am always distracted and how hard it is for her to put up with me. I am sure that today, too, she will voice her grievances in this courtroom. She will blame me for disappearing for the last thirty days and for creating a furore. She will certainly want to know where I was these last thirty days, what I ate, what I did, why I left home. She will go on and on. "What" and "why" she will keep asking… "What" and "why"… A heap of "whats" and "whys"…'

The judge turned to Deepa. 'Do you want to say something?' he asked in a conciliatory tone. She shook her head once again.

The judge then began: 'Though you have laid down your views and grievances in detail and have managed to substantiate them with your observations, you have not stated any specific reason which has compelled you to file a divorce suit. The Court directs that you re-present your case, mentioning your points in order of priority and logical relevance. The Court allows you a period of thirty days to do that.'

Before Nachiketa could think of a reply, the judge spoke again. 'Let me tell you a story. I am sure you have heard it many times before, but listen all the same. A magician once saw a cat chasing a mouse. Feeling pity for the mouse he transformed it into a cat. But he soon noticed that the cat was frightened of dogs and so he turned it into a dog. But, when he saw the dog cowering in front of a lion he metamorphosed it into a lion. He hoped that once it was turned into a lion nothing could frighten the dog. But the sight of a hunter drove the lion into utter panic. The magician was disappointed. He said, "I turned you into a lion, the most ferocious and undaunted amongst all the beasts, but you still remained a mouse within," and returned the creature to its original form.

'You might be wondering how this story is linked to your case. Let me explain. Your arguments may appear to be sound on the surface but are in my opinion mere trifles. Such minor conflicts occur in all marriages. I feel that you are contemplating a divorce when all you both need is private space for yourselves—a long honeymoon. My advice is that you go off on a honeymoon for the next thirty days. You can think about the divorce suit after that. Remember Mr Nachiketa, your whims and your fancies may briefly sustain your life, but you can never transform them into sound logic to justify your actions.'

Fragments

It was almost two hours since Megha had left home. What would Payan have thought? What would he be thinking? First, he would have thought that Megha was out visiting one of their neighbours. Then, he would have thought she was at Ruby-madam's, or Razia-madam's, or even at her father's house. He must have already telephoned several people. The little note she had left behind carried only two brief lines: 'Don't worry. I will be back soon.' Megha had left the note under the thermos—Payan could not have missed it there. He would have read it a number of times and racked his brain to figure out what sort of a surprise Megha had in store for him. He would have smiled, become vexed, then angry, and finally shrugged his shoulders and left for college.

Didn't Payan himself often act in the same way? He would say 'I'll be right back' and go out. Sometimes he would not return till evening. He would have a list of excuses ready for Megha when he returned. He would narrate how he got delayed at the Mukherjees', how he had gone for a swim, or how he had decided to go to the gym. He would complain that his cheekbones were beginning to look prominent; he would rue the fact that he had put on half a kilo. Megha never asked for explanations. She knew Payan was obsessed with cheekbones, shoulder-bones, fitness and things like that. He kept himself perpetually busy toning the muscles of his hands, legs, thighs and chest.

He worked out to keep his cholesterol levels under control and to reduce his paunch. He never sported a moustache or a beard; he would shampoo his hair every day but would never comb it. His favourite God was Apollo, son of Zeus. He had hung a large painting of Apollo on a wall. He used to go on and on about Apollo in such a way that Megha was sometimes tempted to imagine that Payan had himself been Apollo in an earlier life. He was familiar with each and every muscle in Apollo's body.

'You are the goddess of love and wisdom,' Payan would tell Megha. 'You are Athena. You will see how good-looking, strong and intelligent our children will be.'

He no longer spoke about children. Perhaps life would have followed the trajectory Payan had planned had the accident not happened. Megha, too, was no longer interested in babies. They are a great bother, she thought. Megha had seen what Razia-madam had to go through on account of her three children.

All at once Megha stopped in her tracks. She noticed a bull standing in the middle of the road. The animal was at a distance but it did not walk away. She decided she would mingle with pedestrians and walk past the animal. However, there was no pedestrian on the road at that hour—only scooters, cars, trucks and buses raced past. People do not usually walk on highways. So Megha just stood there, carefully watching the bull. After ten minutes or so, a car pulled up near her. Megha saw that a senior colleague of Payan's was at the steering wheel.

'What are you doing here all by yourself?' the man exclaimed. He was clearly surprised at seeing Megha on the highway. 'Where are you headed? Please get in.'

Megha walked round to the door on the other side and got in without a reply. 'I just want to get past that bull,' she murmured.

As soon as the car had driven past the animal, Megha requested the man to stop. 'I shall get down here, sir.'

The professor insisted on driving Megha to her destination. If she was not in a great hurry, she could come over to his house, he suggested—he would inform Payan. But Megha refused the kind-hearted professor's offers. She must get down. She asked the professor to forgive her: 'Not today, sir, please don't mind.' The elderly professor was surprised. Megha did not even go up to the crossroads. She had not travelled even one-tenth of a kilometre in the car. She was not ready to tell him where she was going, either. 'What is the matter with madam Megha?' the professor wondered.

What is the matter with me? Megha wondered.

Payan had gone out for a jog when Megha had left home. She had already taken her bath. She had scribbled a quick note, hung a sling bag over her shoulder and walked out. She had been calm and unperturbed. She had gone to a hotel serving South Indian food and had had a dosa for breakfast. Then, she had bought some sweets and put them in her sling bag. After a cup of tea she had walked to a magazine-stall, where she had bought a copy of *Arts and Ideas*. From the cosmetics shop she had bought a bottle of nail-polish remover. Then she had walked towards the bus stop. The bull had lost her ten minutes; the concerned professor another ten. In all, she had taken about two hours but she managed to catch the bus. It was only 8.30. Only one bus plied between Megha's town and the village she wanted to reach—it left at nine. Megha wanted to catch that bus but had not told anyone of her plan.

She looked outside to see if she knew anyone at the bus stop. She saw Tripathy-sir, their neighbour, with his baby daughter, Pia. The little girl was genuinely fond of Megha. Pia would call out to her enthusiastically and run to her whenever she caught sight of Megha. Megha, too, liked Pia a lot. She felt tempted to call out to her but restrained herself, fearing questions from Pia's father. She turned away and looked in the opposite direction. After twenty minutes or so the driver came in and took his seat. Megha must have looked at her watch twenty times in twenty minutes.

What would Payan be doing now? Megha wondered. Had Professor Mukherjee called him and told him about meeting Megha? If he had, Payan must have gone out again to look for her. What was he thinking? She had never done such a thing in the seven years and seven months that they had been married.

~

After the rape, Payan had taken great care of Megha. His love for her had grown even more intense after the incident. Payan's colleagues, students, neighbours, friends and relatives—everyone had treated Megha with care and sensitivity, they had showered their love and affection upon her. The principal was himself monitoring her case. But the case had been held up because Mahadeva, the culprit, was displaying signs of madness.

Megha had never set eyes on Mahadeva, either before or after those fateful fifteen or twenty minutes. During these last few months, though, she had been gripped by a strange curiosity: she wanted to see the man and to learn about his family, his wife and children. What happened to the woman after her husband was sent to jail? How was she running her family? Megha was curious, too, about what Mahadeva was doing in jail. What was he thinking? Did he feel remorse? Was he still in an unbalanced state of mind? Why did he commit such a heinous act? Megha had once confided to Payan that she wanted to meet her rapist. Payan's reaction had bordered on the violent.

'What nonsense! Are you out of your mind? How can you think of such a thing? How can you meet your rapist?' Megha's uncle, who was a doctor; the principal of Payan's college; as well as a few senior colleagues of Payan's had also tried to dissuade her when they had heard; they had asked her to never entertain such an outrageous idea. But Megha could not forget, nor could she crush her curiosity. She had become obsessed with the idea over these last two months. It was to fulfil this secret desire which had been haunting her almost every moment that she had, on an impulse, walked out of the house.

No one, not even Payan himself, could have linked this to Megha's absence.

~

Megha's maternal uncle and his wife were both gynaecologists of repute. After Megha had failed to conceive even after five years of marriage, Payan and Megha had consulted the doctor couple. Following their advice, Payan and Megha had had their chromosomes tested. They had undergone the Mantoux Test, the semen test and the microbe-count test. Megha had undergone a D&C test and an HSG test. The doctor couple had explained to them about the stoma and the Fallopian tubes. The tests revealed that everything was in order. Her aunt had drawn a diagram of the female reproductive organ and explained the position of the ovaries, the Fallopian tubes and their function; she had also told her about the fourteen-day fertility cycle and finally given Megha a broad smile and wished her luck. Still, Megha had not conceived. At times she had thought it would be easier to adopt a baby from the Child Welfare Department. Why go to all that trouble? Megha tried to reason with herself. How people stared at the progressive growth of a pregnant woman's belly—what a vulgar look they had in their eyes! Megha felt relieved that at least she and Payan were within a circle of safety where such things could not hurt them.

~

The bus reached Megha's destination in an hour. She alighted and looked around. A group of four men and two women stared at her. She asked one of them for Mahadeva Behera's address. They shook their heads. After whispering among themselves, three of them asked together: 'The Mahadeva who is in jail?' Then one of them pointed to a house in the distance and said, 'That is the village hall, his wife lives in the bus-stop adjacent to that hall. But what do you want to meet her for?'

Megha did not answer, she only thanked them and walked towards the club-house. She stood in front of the shed which once used to function as a bus-stop and which had now been converted into a house with the help of bamboo mats and bamboo posts. The front wall and the door were made up of split bamboo—the door had only a latch. As Megha was about to knock,

someone called out from a distance, 'Push it open, they
may be inside.' Megha gingerly pushed the door open and
stepped within. A small girl and a woman, who Megha
thought must be the girl's mother, were sleeping on a cot.
The sound of the door had woken them and both of them
sat up. Megha noticed that the room was very small—it
measured no more than eight feet by eight feet, and the
roof was very low.

A rope that had once served to draw water in buckets
from a well now functioned as a clothesline from which
were hung a tattered, thin mattress; torn sheets; empty
sacks; a shabby-looking sweater; a frock; dirty saris and
blouses; and a stained towel. A small box under the cot,
some aluminium utensils, a few glass bottles and a tin
kerosene lamp seemed to be the family's only material
possessions. A vegetable basket lay on the floor; it
contained a few dried-up green chillies, onion peels, a
vegetable-cutter with a sitting-board, two rubber dolls
and a stack of old newspapers. There was a hearth at one
corner near the head of the cot. Megha could see some
half-burnt pieces of wood inside the hearth on which
some milk had spilt. On the hearth sat an earthen pot.
An earthen pitcher of water stood by the hearth; beside
it were four tin containers, a plastic bucket, a book for
primary-school students and a slate. The torn, curled-up
pages on both sides of the book gave it a semi-circular
shape.

Megha sat down on the narrow cement veranda. 'Are
you Sulapi?' she asked.

'Yes.'

'My name is Meghamala. Have you heard of me?'

'No.'

'Who reads this book and writes on the slate?'

'No one. My daughter plays with them.'

'You have never heard of me? Doesn't the name Meghamala strike a chord?'

'No.'

'About a year back your husband …'

Abruptly, Sulapi moved to the vegetable basket, took out the newspapers and dusted them. She showed Megha her husband's photograph printed in one of the pages and the report under it.

'This?' she asked and watched Megha curiously.

'Yes. I am the victim.'

Sulapi was stunned. Then she broke into tears and cried like a child. Megha said nothing. She gave the little girl a chocolate. She also took out a sweet from her sling bag and gave it to her. The girl stopped crying. But Sulapi kept weeping. She could not think of a single reason that could have made Megha come to her house. In a soft but persuasive manner, Megha tried to extract from Sulapi information about her husband, her house and her family. She asked Sulapi how she was managing on her own. She also asked her about Mahadeva. She wanted to know how long Sulapi had known him. She wanted to know if there had been any noticeable change in Mahadeva's behaviour just before the incident.

Something in Megha's demeanour prompted Sulapi to open the secret pages of her life to her, and she took Megha into her past.

Both Mahadeva and Sulapi lived in the same village but they did not belong to the same caste. Each day, Mahadeva and Sulapi would attend school four kilometres from their village along with other children. Mahadeva never took the usual route to the school; he preferred, instead, to walk through the jungle, plucking wild berries and exotic flowers. He would never mix with the girls nor would he talk to them or tease them like other boys of his age. He would climb up to the top branches of the trees, pluck berries and throw them down so that he could collect them after climbing down. He would get infuriated if the girls picked up the berries he had thrown down. He had not spoken a word to Sulapi, or indeed, to any other girl during the two years he spent in school. One afternoon, Sulapi picked up a leti, a ripe mango, which Mahadeva had thrown down. She tried to run away before Mahadeva could get down but Mahadeva chased her and beat her black and blue. Thereafter, he stopped coming to school. He left the village that very night. Nobody knew he had gone to Raipur by train until he returned after two months. He did not go back to school; instead, he tried his hand at different kinds of work. He worked as a waiter in a hotel, a helper in a kerosene shop, a bellboy at a lodge and as a mechanic, but could not stick to any job. He was driven out from everywhere. He would buy artificial pearl necklaces, bangles, ribbons and saris for Sulapi when things went well between them. She, too, would accept the gifts, putting behind her the memories of the cruel beatings he used to shower on her. Finally, Mahadeva and Sulapi left the village one day without telling anyone. They went to a small town some two hundred kilometres away and started working in a textile mill there.

They lived together as husband and wife, carried heavy bales of cloth, and shouldered all the burdens of life. After an extensive search, his family eventually traced them to the textile mill. It took a lot of persuasion to bring Mahadeva and Sulapi back to their village.

Mahadev's father kept him locked inside a room. One night, he opened the back door, released Mahadeva and left with him for Raipur. Sulapi thought Mahadeva was behind the locked door, pining for her. From morning to evening, she would sit in the courtyard of Mahadeva's house. She bore the fiery stings of the vulgar abuses hurled at her, she patiently bore the beatings Mahadeva's mother and sister gave her, but refused to leave. In the evenings she would go back home. There, again, she had to patiently bear the beatings and rebuke of her parents and sister. She did not complain. She ate a bowl of watery rice once or twice a day to sustain the life that was growing inside her womb. After ten days of anguish she came to know that Mahadeva had already disappeared from behind the locked door.

He did not return until after two years. Sulapi was admitted to the hospital in due course and delivered a girl child. She named her daughter Amari. Sulapi and her baby daughter were refused shelter even by Sulapi's own family. That was when she had come away to this village with her baby and started earning her livelihood working as a domestic help. She made fuel-cakes from cowdung at someone's house, washed utensils at someone else's, and fetched water for someone else. She struggled hard to keep herself and her daughter alive. She thrived on her own struggles. She came across a number of men who unabashedly professed their love for her but ignored them. She survived on her own. She volunteered to help other poor women who earned their livelihood by selling roasted rice or pounding parboiled paddy at the husking-pedal.

Not even once did her parents turn up to see how their daughter was doing. Though Sulapi's younger sister paid occasional visits to her house, and brought chocolates and fruits for Amari.

Her life had fallen into a pattern when Sulapi learnt about Mahadeva's arrest. She came to know that he had been charged with raping a woman. The police had beaten him mercilessly and he was in hospital, she had learnt. She had stored the newspaper which had carried a photograph of Mahadeva and narrated the incident.

Megha put down the chocolates and sweets on the veranda and rose to her feet. 'I shall leave now, but you have no reason to fear. I came to visit you just out of curiosity,' she said. Her voice carried a note of assurance. She took out a hundred-rupee note from her purse and gave it to Sulapi. 'Keep it,' she said and left.

Megha headed straight to jail. It was ten kilometres from Sulapi's village. From the highway, she would have to board a town bus in order to reach the jail where Mahadeva was lodged. He had been transferred to a single cell in the jail hospital. Megha met the jailor and was led to Mahadeva's room.

She gingerly pushed the door open and looked in; the jailer, too, peered in. Mahadeva stood facing the opposite wall. He was quiet. 'He stands like this for hours, staring at the wall,' the jailor said. 'Mahadeva! Mahadeva!' he called out. Mahadeva turned and looked at his visitors. He did not react in any way when he saw Megha.

'Sit down, Mahadeva,' the jailor said. 'See who has come to meet you.' Mahadeva took a seat on the cot but did not look at them. 'Do you recognize this lady?' the jailor asked. Mahadeva did not say anything. Megha took out a small photograph from her purse and handed it to the jailor. She gestured to suggest that the jailor should hand Mahadeva her photograph. Mahadeva stared at the photo for a long time then tore it to pieces and flung them on to the ground. After some time he picked up one of the pieces and gazed at it. It was an eye. He then began picking up the pieces one after another and tried to arrange them properly, like someone trying to solve a jigsaw puzzle. When the pieces fell into place, Mahadeva screamed wildly. Terrified, Megha ran out of the room. Perhaps Mahadeva had recognized Megha from the torn fragments. He was panting. He did not stop screaming even though he was gasping for breath. The jailor tried to stop him but failed. So excited had the man become that he jumped about across the room and, with a violent sweep of his hand, flung down the bottles of medicines kept on the shelf, smashing them into pieces. He lifted the trolley of medicine and brought it down with a violent crash. As he charged at Megha, four attendants held him back. They put him back on the bed and kept his hands and legs pinned to it while the nurse injected a sedative. Mahadeva went to sleep soon after. 'No more of this, let's leave,' the jailor declared. Megha accompanied him to his office.

There, the jailor revealed some astonishing details about Mahadeva's erratic behaviour. Mahadeva did not seem to comprehend full sentences but could understand fragmented ones. The sound of a bomb exploding would not disturb him but the rustle of a broom sweeping the floor could make him restless. He could not stand the fragrance of incense, the smell of phenol or any other disinfectant. Even the smell of medicine seemed to suffocate him. The sight of dead creatures would agitate him. He would be very disturbed by the sight of a lizard, a mouse or a sparrow getting caught in the moving blades of the ceiling fan and being brought down.

Sometimes, even the most powerful sedatives would fail to calm him. He would become delirious when he saw dogs and sparrows fornicating outside the window. He would become so violent at the sight that people would immediately move aside to safety. Some people, however, would manage to grab him and pin him down. Mahadeva would struggle fiercely, sweat streaming down his body, but he would finally be subdued.

Megha could not take any more of this. 'I will leave now,' she said and rose to her feet. The jailor offered her some coffee and refreshments. Megha refused the refreshments, accepted the coffee, thanked the jailor and left.

It was evening when she came out of the jail. She looked at her wristwatch but could not figure out the time in the dark. It took Megha nearly an hour to reach home. From a distance, she saw a crowd of people standing near her house. A car and about a dozen scooters and motorbikes were parked there. The crowd and the vehicles made her uncomfortable. Her heart throbbed in fear.

'Has some accident taken place?'

'No,' someone answered, and Megha was relieved.

All the people gathered were anxiously waiting for Megha. The crowd included her parents, some of Payan's colleagues, her doctor uncle and aunt, Razia-madam, Ruby-madam, Mukerjee-sir and several of her neighbours. There they stood, waiting for her. Payan looked at her questioningly.

'Where were you?' he asked.

'I met Mahadeva and Sulapi please don't ask me anything more I have only one request I wish to withdraw the case Now please leave me alone.'

Megha said all of this in one breath and went inside.

The Alphabet Garden

(For a three-month-old left to die
in a brick kiln)

THE COSMOS IS born of a story,
A story which once carried a handful of vapour within
itself like a crumpled spiderweb.
Within the vapour, a womb;
Within the womb, a drop of immortal blood;
Within the blood, a molecule of inexorable semen;
Within the semen, a seed, atom-sized:
That seed, that atom, held my Being.
For aeons I revolved, whirlwind-like, around the
seed-atom;
I was the nucleus in the atom,
The seed in the semen,
The life in the seed.
After countless revolutions, my Being took shape:
First an oval, an ellipse, Mother Earth, the letter 'O',
Then a slit—my mouth,
Then the first sound—my cry,
Then letters, words,

Then fire, heat and light,

Then two tiny holes—my nose. They inhale, and exhale—storm, hurricane, thunderbolt, lightning,

Then two projections of flesh on my head—my ears. They heard sounds, music—a symphony. From the symphony were born the solar system, the planets, the satellites and the stars.

Soon after, a membrane spread over my Being—my skin. The touch, the contraction and expansion of it. The down which sprouted upon it and created the trees, the forests, the gardens, the flowers, the buds, the pollen, the colours, the fragrance.

A beat within my Being—a tiny heart, very light, very lovely, very neat. From the heart was born the moon, the sky—moonlit, star-studded—dawn, dusk, the tides and the waves.

A whirlpool—my navel. The cord which linked the navel all the way down to earth.

A knob of flesh below the navel—my penis. Semen gurgled out of it, and water. From the water emerged an ocean and clouds and rain and flood and deluge.

Finally, a pair of twinkling eyes—sight was born. Scenes flashed before them—scenes from a world of fantasy, a land of dreams, light and darkness.

I was now fully formed,

The entire universe lay open in front of me.

How had I fit into a seed, a nucleus, a molecule of semen, a drop of blood, a womb, a ball of vapour? My

mouth, my eyes, my ears, my nose, my navel, my penis—
how did they fit into that cloud?

My voice, my vision, my senses of touch, smell,
hearing—where in that celestial vapour did they reside?

My hunger, my desire to weep, my libido, my passion
to learn, my urge to live… How had that vapour held my
vows, my sacrifices, my soul, my passions?

How could a drop of semen hold the hot-spring of my
body, the pulsing blood of my veins, my urine, my bile,
my phlegm, my saliva, my sweat, my tears? Where in that
drop of semen was my horoscope? How did it carry the
details of the star I was born under?

Witness the miserable plight of my bones, my limbs
which constantly kicked at the sky from within the drop
of semen.

Witness the plight of my blood, my tears, my sweat,
my saliva—all crammed into a semen-drop which rose
and fell like waves in the sea.

Witness the tragic outcome of my unfulfilled desire to
drink my mother's milk; my inexorable efforts to remain
glued to her breasts.

Witness the fate of the three unfortunate smiles which
lit up my face three times in three months.

Witness how the five bulls of my senses ransacked
this beautiful garden.

How lovely was that garden—its bone-fence, the
hothouse shaded by milky-white skin, the pulsing
channels of arteries and veins, the graceful spinal cord,

miniscule lumps of flesh—lying in wait for the god-seed. What a beautiful dream it was. A god-tree would rise in the garden, a divine scarecrow. Eight-armed, adorned with bangle, bracelet, flowers; bearing conch, bugle, arms. What a beautiful dream it was. How beautiful that primordial cry.

But the fire-eating devils would not let the garden grow, would they? They herded their five bulls in. They invaded through its five doors—the eyes, the skin, the tongue, the nose and ears. They stampeded, trampled the sprouts, tore the tender branches off, dug the earth with their horns and wrought havoc. They screamed and bellowed with my voice. The heat of their rage dried up the ocean of milk within me. They devastated the tender hothouse and shrank my three-month-long life into a film that lasted merely three hours. The devils enjoyed only one scene in that three-hour film: the one in which I cried; my cries, my screams, my moans, my tortured groans were what they revelled in.

I cried for three long hours—my tiny hands and feet kicked at the sky. The clouds cracked and lightning streaked through them; my mouth opened and closed as I screamed.

The stars and planets were flung about; my breath fanned tornadoes. My five vital airs—the air of life, prana; the air of my anus, apana; the air of my navel, samana; the air underneath my feet, udana; the air of my belly, byana—produced thunder and lightning. A flood of tears flowed endlessly from my staring eyes; my dying hiccups had the power to smash mountains to pieces.

The film went on. The devils laughed and guffawed. They clapped and rejoiced. 'What flawless acting! Romantic, adventurous, poetic!' they shouted in joy.

Then my body fell silent, shrank, and the sap of life leached out of it. I lay coiled in sleep and the film rolled to its end. The devils whistled and roared with laughter; sitting on the deer-throne, they masturbated.

I slept; no, I lay in a fortress of unbaked bricks. The earth, connected to my navel with the cord, sucked away the vital essence of my life. A long, long line of ants which seemed to have emerged out of Infinity itself reached up to it.

Unbaked bricks stacked one over the other in an endless wall, like darkness piled layer upon layer. Shafts of light penetrate gaps in the wall.

At a great height, a ragged piece of sky... In the three months Eternity granted me, I never saw a single bird fly across that fragment of sky. Never even a scrap of light, fluffy cloud that might have floated away from a larger one.

The sky, or the part of it I could see, was always hot and dry.

Man-made bricks and brick-hard men invaded the fortress of brick. They were sturdy and rough, and their faces wore a brick-hard look. Their hands were rugged and ugly, and their skin had peeled off. Those brick-hard faces leaned close and the brick-hands caressed my cheeks, my lips, my back and my belly. No wonder they bled. It was dreadful, like a tender mouse-pup being patted by a lion.

On very rare occasions, a shadow would come, a shadow as smooth as butter. Its touch was very tender, very cool, like cotton wool or powdered ice, perhaps a sponge. It had a very soft voice, wet and suffused with emotion. The shadow would lend its soft, cool touch to the entire expanse of my garden. But the devil would always shove the shadow away and fling it into the depths of a black abyss. The shadow would shrink and become invisible. It disappeared among the other shadows and finally melted into the ether.

One day, a devil dragged me deep into a forest. With a pair of scissors it tore my body into two; from my penis to my chest and from my chest to my shoulders. He examined the insides of my body, tried to find out what it was made of. He searched with care, seeking this thing we call sorrow. He dug the earth, moved aside the creepers, wrenched out the roots, but could not find it. Frustrated, he dumped everything back into my body and, with rough hands, stitched up the thin curtain which wrapped the hothouse; it was as if he was sewing a sack of potatoes. He dumped me back in the fortress and stealthily left. No one knew who had done it. The men of brick no longer touched me, nor did the shadows care any longer to keep me cool. Everyone was shocked and felt compelled to stay away from me.

The cosmos was born out of a story,
The story has come to its end.
I am no more,
My very essence has evaporated.

My cries, once the greatest gift of Nature, have become abhorrent. I can no longer be neatly folded and placed among the brick stacks.

The shadows closed in, shrouded me in a cool mantle and floated me away in a holy drain.

The bricks were forbidden to cry. They only whispered—Remember how we men of brick and the devils who prod us here strip off our old clothes and put on new ones? You, primal child, shed your old body, the one that has been sewn up like a sack of potatoes, and take on a new one. Your Being cannot be destroyed by any weapon nor can fire burn it; water cannot drown it, wind cannot blow it away.

Nothing can touch you anymore,
You are eternal and omnipresent;
You are infinite.
You exist as Mother Earth, as the letter 'O'.
Each day, you die a fresh death,
Each day, you are born anew.
You are shanti, shanti, shanti.

Translator's Note

'TRANSLATION IS A contract, a recognition of obligation which requires the "authentic other" to be created anew in a new language and in a new culture but in the exact image, tone and texture of the original' writes Sreedevi K. Nair in her note to the English rendition of S.K. Pottekkatt's Malayalam text Tales of *Athiranippadam*.

The translator is, in a way, the author of the 'authentic other' because the 'authentic other' is an altogether different framework—though mirror-like—wherein are fitted the reflections of the original. The legitimacy of the translated text's claim for autonomy, no doubt, depends largely on its readability and aesthetic appeal. The translator's commitment, her involvement in the task and of course her competence and honesty to the pledge to deliver the pure and the right stuff are elemental so that the new text gains artistic charm and effectiveness.

A translator's role—as is often postulated—could be compared to that of an artist; for example, a musician or an actor who interprets a work of art. Like other arts, translation inescapably involves choice and choice implies interpretation. The need to interpret is even more urgent in the act of translating a literary text from a source language like Odia because the translation has to be not only bi-lingual, but also bi-cultural; for language is not merely a collection of words and rules of grammar but a vast, interconnected system of connotations and cultural references.

All these put together makes a translator's task unquestionably a demanding one, besides being engaging and challenging, depending upon the nature of the text to be translated and the degree of receptivity of its readers.

The first reading of Manoj Panda's work in Odia compels us to wonder why these stories, which so skilfully wield the themes of existentialism, isolation and the predicament of man living in alienation in a hostile world; stories which exhibit the excellence of the writer's innovative experimentation with structural patterns and, are, in the poet Professor Soubhagya K. Mishra's opinion, 'the finest stories in Odia', need to be replicated in English. The translator would obviously feel a degree of skepticism in taking up the task of ensuring 'exactitude' which is bound to be missing in the 'authentic other', though that exactitude will be expected of the translation, particularly by readers conversant with both the source and the receptor languages.

The three major strands which have been used to weave the intricate fabric of these stories are the themes, the style, and the typical culture-specific language system which bears the obvious 'Manoj Panda' stamp and which seems to hover threateningly on the edge of untranslatability. Translating his writing into English, is bound to, as is pointed out by some esteemed critics, scrape off a sizeable slice of the typical Manoj Panda touch which lends his Odia stories their separate, distinctive identity. But no sensible translator, in my opinion, would prefer to compromise with the Odianess of the stories had there been an alternative. The translator's big hope, therefore, rests on the indisputable truth that English is a very powerful language and will not fail to contain all the strands which make up Panda's stories.

~

Amongst the themes the author chooses, the one of foremost importance is man's compulsive urge to battle the inexorability of an unpitying destiny, as reflected in tales like 'Kaniska', 'One Thousand Days in a Refrigerator' and 'A Picture of Agony'. They express a profound despondence at the mockery human life becomes in its rebellious, impotent fight with an invincible destiny. 'The Aesthetics of a Supercyclone' is a poignant tale of self-discovery while 'The Hunt', 'When the Gods Left' and 'Filling in the Blanks' illustrate the plight of human beings trapped in coercive and repressive socio-moral-economic systems.

These stories, like paintings, describe a melancholic picture of man on an ever-expanding canvas of pain and despair, and at the same time reveal his inner strength, his eternal struggle to survive the odds, and his indomitable passion to exist with dignity even as he is pitted against a system that is destined to wipe out his very existence. Running through all the stories is a faint, but consistent, strain of mild sarcasm tinged with a note of pathos and bleak humour.

These are no ordinary stories which aim solely at entertaining the reader. They are the observations of a skilled mind-reader which delve into multiple layers of human behaviour to examine the consuming passions there and to find the real 'self'. At the end of most of the stories the reader might find himself confounded by the unsolved puzzles of life which the author, like a deft and experienced conjuror, holds out.

Manoj Kumar Panda has a style all his own: a fusion of prosaic sentences interspersed with lines of free verse, all of which combine to form an 'aesthetics of the bizarre' which, in the view of some critics, is a phrase that best describes many of his stories. A note of pathos juxtaposed with one of mild sarcasm to generate dark humour is another hallmark of Panda's style. Yet another hallmark are quick shifts in tense–the narrative glides from the present to an immediate past, then to a distant and remote one, and again flows back to the present.

A post-modernist in approach through and through, Manoj Panda stresses upon narrative structure to communicate experiences emerging out of a proximity with a reality that is too harsh to be represented otherwise. He is, it appears, out to build a world of symbols to depict effectively the anguished cry of the soul for liberation from the cage of self-created convictions, dogma and a formula-ridden society. The many-faceted symbolism employed, which at times borders on a lexical puzzle, admits more interpretation than one. One that is tricky to transfer in a balanced and poised manner to English.

Making observations on his own style Panda says, 'No dictionary can help us to find the meaning of a word, because there is no such thing as meaning.' In other words, no word has a final, specific meaning; it can have only connotations, and a word can have several connotations, each slightly varying from the other depending upon its contextual position in a given sentence or passage. This might perhaps be the reason why the author chooses to create his own lexicon, where a word can have any number of significations.

'The path that is supposed to lead towards meaning is a jagged, mysterious one,' the author says further. 'It's like a spiral track that spins round and round like the insides of a whirlpool, and it is always possible for the meaning to get sucked in by the violent surge of emotions generated in that bottomless depth...'

The author's views greatly influence the translator's task, since the primary duty of a translator is to seek out and interpret the deep-rooted thought embedded in the text, the 'invariant core' as Andre Lefevere terms it, and at the same time to differentiate between the level of emotional experience and the emotion-concept while expressing them in English, since certain emotion-concepts may appear foreign to the readers in the receptor language. In the words of theorists Fehr and Russell, 'everyday concepts do not refer directly to the emotional sphere, but to a representational level by which emotional experience is categorized depending on the degree of similarity with a mental script'. Hence the task of appropriate transference of everyday concept of emotions or ideas entails the establishing of a cross-cultural comparison even as the relationship between the normal concept and the emotional experience is analyzed. While translating the stories, it had to be borne in mind translation equivalents might not express exactly the same concept, though most of the cross-cultural comparison of emotion-concepts has relied on emotion-terms and one-to-one translation. There is, all the same, no sharp boundary between the two and they represent rather a spectrum of translational approaches. It is the modus operandi that varies from translator to translator or conditioned by the nature of the text to be translated that chooses to keep them apart or attempts a judicious blending of the two.

A translated text is obviously not meant to be a complete transformation of the original, but is a semantically, pragmatically and dynamically equivalent one because a translation is confronted with the range of interpretabilities of a given text, and the translator's task is to analyze consciously the superstructure of the context embossed on a complex texture of language.

The translator's plight is crucial while she is at the task of recasting the stories in English, stories that are bold experiments in 'form', written in a style that refuses to conform to the traditional or familiar formulae of expression. The translator has to not only familiarize herself with Panda's lexical innovativeness and the inevitable semantic and syntactic ambiguity resulting from it, but has to discretely and judiciously select matching words, terms, and nuances to re-write the stories with utmost loyalty to the original work, without tampering even distantly with the 'invariant core' of the source text, and preserving at the same time its beauty and elegance in the words and style and mode of expression of the other language.

While at the task, I have tried to put in my best possible effort to conform to certain indispensable and basic norms of replicating a text in another language, and at the same time to retain its effectiveness and literary appeal as far as possible. I hope I have not drastically failed in imbuing the spirit of the original in the 'other' text meant for the 'other' set of readers.

Acknowledgements

I EXPRESS MY deep sense of gratitude both to the translator of these stories, Snehaprava Das, and to the editor at Speaking Tiger, Anurag Basnet, for their painstaking endeavours without which this book wouldn't be a possibility. I am also grateful to Professor Jatindra K. Nayak for granting permission, on behalf of Rupantar Publication, Bhubaneswar, to republish my stories translated by Snehaprava. I also acknowledge the existence of some of my characters, Lara, Megha, Premashila, Hiran Majhi, Rajula Dip, Kaniska and others, who have kept me alive all these years.

—MKP